Nv

Declan decided he would use himself as bait to seduce Olivia away from Jeremy.

He found it well-nigh incredible that someone as basically worthless as Jeremy should have two women desperate to spend their lives with him. But it was clear that all was not perfect in the Garden of Eden, so he'd see what a little concentrated temptation could do. Find out if he could lead Olivia astray. Beguile her into falling in love a little.

He'd be doing her a favor, after all, because he couldn't see any future for Olivia with Jeremy—even if Jeremy's wife gave up the struggle and divorced him. And he wouldn't do any lasting damage, he told himself defensively, as he stripped off his clothes.

All the same, a persistent image of her— the vulnerable slant of her neck and shoulders as she'd sat in front of that damned computer—kept coming into his mind. Haunting him....

The streets of London aren't just paved
with gold—they're home to three of the
world's most eligible bachelors!

NOTTING HILL GROOMS

London, England: a city of style, sophistication—
and romance! Its exclusive Notting Hill district is
the perfect place to fall in love. Sparks fly as
three sexy, single men meet—and marry—three
lively, independent women....

This fabulous new miniseries features the talents
of Sara Craven, Mary Lyons and
Sophie Weston: three hugely popular
authors who between them have sold more
than 35 million books worldwide.

Other books in this series are:

On sale Jan. 2000:
Reform of the Playboy#2083 by Mary Lyons
On sale Feb. 2000:
The Millionaire Affair #2089 by Sophie Weston

SARA CRAVEN

Irresistible Temptation

NOTTING HILL GROOMS

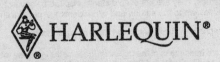

HARLEQUIN®

TORONTO • NEW YORK • LONDON
AMSTERDAM • PARIS • SYDNEY • HAMBURG
STOCKHOLM • ATHENS • TOKYO • MILAN • MADRID
PRAGUE • WARSAW • BUDAPEST • AUCKLAND

ISBN 0-373-12077-X

IRRESISTIBLE TEMPTATION

First North American Publication 2000.

Copyright © 1999 by Sara Craven.

Visit us at www.romance.net

Printed in U.S.A.

CHAPTER ONE

'THIS train is now approaching Paddington. Will passengers make sure they take their luggage and all personal possessions with them?'

Olivia swallowed as the announcement came over the system, her fingers tightening round the strap of her bag. She rose, made her way along the swaying carriage to the luggage rack at the far end, and retrieved her suitcase. She'd been on edge throughout the journey, and now that it was almost over her stomach was churning with nervous excitement.

It's all right, she told herself. Very soon now you'll be with Jeremy, and everything will be fine. This is what you want. What you've dreamed of. And all you have to do is—go for it.

She took the slip of paper from her pocket, and glanced at it again. 16 Lancey Gardens, W11, she repeated soundlessly to herself for the umpteenth time.

'That's the Ladbroke Grove area in Notting Hill,' Beth, her more knowledgeable flatmate had told her, brows lifted. 'Very swish.'

'He's got a marvellous job,' Olivia said proudly. 'He can afford it.'

'There's nothing the matter with your job.' Beth gave her a measuring look. 'So why pack it all in and go chasing rainbows—in the Smoke?'

'You know why.' Olivia began transferring neat piles of undies and nightwear from the chest of drawers to the open case on the bed.

'Livvy—he's a married man, for God's sake.'

'Some marriage—with her in Bristol and him in

5

London,' Olivia retorted. 'Beth—it's over; believe me. It's been dead for more than a year now. They want different things. She's totally wrapped up in her career. Didn't I show you that piece in the paper announcing she'd just been made a partner in her law firm?'

'Which only proves she's doing well. Wives are allowed to, you know. It's not a male prerogative any more.' Beth's tone was dry. 'Anyway, it doesn't give you *carte blanche* to pursue her husband to London.'

'Jeremy and I want to be together,' Olivia insisted. 'And it's time we took positive steps to achieve this.'

'Is that how Jeremy sees it?' Beth's look of mild enquiry metamorphosed into a frown. 'My God, Livvy. You have told him you're joining him? Haven't you?'

'Not exactly,' Olivia said defensively. 'But it was always understood that we'd be together in London. It was just a question of timing. And, with Maria getting her partnership, this is clearly the time.'

'He's been in London for three months. Shouldn't you have got together at some point? Discussed things?'

Olivia shrugged. 'He's been busy—settling into a new job—new flat. We talk on the phone—and write.'

'You write,' said Beth. 'He phones—sometimes.'

Olivia's mouth tightened. 'You don't really like Jeremy, do you?'

'I haven't any feelings about him either way.' Beth was dismissive. 'But I don't like what he's doing to you. The games he's playing.'

'I don't know what you mean.' Olivia tucked tissue into the folds of a black skirt.

'Yes, you do, but clearly you don't want to talk about it. So I'll just say this—if I was going with a guy, I'd want a bit more out of the relationship than a few vague promises of eternal bliss—some time.' Beth's tone was edged.

Olivia flushed. 'If you're talking about sex...'

'Which I am.'

'Then we want that too, of course, but it didn't seem

right. Not while he was still living here in Bristol with Maria. Now the separation is official, we can—make our own commitment to each other.'

'Such passion,' Beth commented wryly.

'It's not just an affair,' Olivia insisted. 'We want to build a life together—a home—ultimately a family. My joining him in London is the first step on the way.'

'Then I hope it all works out for you, I really do.' Beth gave her a swift hug. 'But I won't advertise your room immediately—just in case...'

Remembering, Olivia frowned as she hefted her case along the platform, and out on to the main concourse. The train had been crowded, mostly, she suspected, with Saturday shoppers, and she had to thread her way through a mass of people to find the taxi rank.

Beth means well, she thought, taking her place in the queue, and setting her case down thankfully. But she doesn't really know Jeremy. Not like I do.

There hardly seemed a time when he hadn't been part of her life. They'd grown up in the same Somerset village, and Olivia had always been slightly in awe of his blond good looks, and the assurance bestowed by his six years' seniority over her. She'd been shyly happy when he'd come home for the school holidays, however little attention he'd paid her, and she'd grieved silently when he'd left for university.

During his second year away, his parents had sold their house and moved to a smaller property on the coast, and she'd decided sadly that she'd never see him again.

Their meeting last year in a Bristol wine bar had been the purest coincidence. She'd been there with a colleague from work, unwinding after a long, hard day teaching computerised office systems to a particularly unreceptive bunch of secretaries.

Jeremy had been with a crowd of people at a leaving do on the other side of the room. The wine bar had been full, and not particularly well-lit, but she'd recognised him at

once. Heard him laugh. Had seen his brilliant smile flash
as he'd turned to trade cheerful insults with another member of his party.

When he'd gone up to the bar, she'd followed. Touched
his sleeve…

'Hello, Jeremy. I don't expect you remember me…'

He turned, brows lifting in sudden hauteur, which disappeared like the sun breaking through clouds as he registered her presence.

'Livvy Butler—by all that's wonderful. I don't believe
it. How long has it been?'

Too long, she thought, bathed in the warmth of that
smile. Basking, for once, in his undivided attention.

'You look terrific.' His blue eyes took in everything,
from the streaked brown hair enhanced by a fortnight in
the Greek sun, to the pink enamel on the toenails peeping
from her chic, high-heeled sandals. He glanced round. 'Are
you with someone, or can we talk?'

'I was just leaving…'

'No, don't do that. Look, those people in the corner are
going. Grab their table while I get us a drink. Is Chardonnay all right?'

She'd have drunk wolfsbane if he'd offered it to her.

Moments later, they were sitting at the corner table, and
he was pouring wine into her glass.

'Are you sure your friends won't mind?' she asked
doubtfully.

Jeremy shrugged. 'I've done my duty. The way things
are going, my absence won't even be noticed.' He handed
over her glass. Raised his own in a toast. 'Happy meetings,
Livvy. Tell me, what are you doing in Bristol?'

Waiting for you, she thought, as she raised her glass in
turn. But I never knew it until this moment…

The taxi queue shuffled up, and Olivia shuffled with it,
impatience building inside her. Why couldn't all these people wanting Harrods or Selfridges share each other's cabs,
and save their money and her precious time?

Now that she was here, she wanted to be with Jeremy. Needed to see his face light up with incredulity and delight, and his arms opening wide to enfold her.

When it had started, it had been purely platonic. Just two old friends meeting for the odd drink—the occasional meal. Jeremy had made no secret of the fact that he was married, and she'd respected him for that.

She couldn't remember the moment when she first registered that all might not be well in his marriage. Jeremy always spoke with pride of his wife's career achievements, but was reticent—even tight-lipped—about their personal relationship, and gradually she'd found herself wondering.

Then, one day, he'd rung her at work and asked almost abruptly if she'd have dinner with him that evening. When she'd arrived at the restaurant, she'd found a candlelit table for two, and champagne waiting on ice.

'It's my birthday,' he'd told her quietly. 'Unfortunately, my wife is too busy preparing a major case for the Crown Court to come out with me. Thanks for making time for me, Livvy.'

Over the evening, Jeremy had spoken openly about his marriage for the first time.

'With Maria, the job comes first, second and third,' he'd said bitterly. 'I'm not even sure I end up a poor fourth.'

'That can't be true.' She'd put her hand over his. 'You've been married such a short time. You have to talk it out—reach some kind of compromise...'

'How can you talk to someone who won't admit there's a problem?' He'd shaken his head. 'I'm not certain we've ever had a marriage at all.' His fingers had closed round hers. 'I should have waited, Livvy,' he'd said huskily. 'Waited for you. I know that now. Tell me it's not too late.'

'Wake up, love.' The taxi driver's strident voice broke impatiently into her reverie. 'Do you want a cab or not?'

'Oh, yes.' Red-faced, Olivia gave him her destination and heaved her case on board, collapsing back on to the seat as the cab moved off.

She hardly knew London at all, she reflected. Her only previous visits had been brief sightseeing trips when she was much younger. Living here would be a totally different matter.

She was used to heavy traffic in Bristol, but it didn't compare with the sheer volume confronting her now. The cab was crawling along, hemmed in by other vehicles, only occasionally diving through some tiny gap, as if making a bid for freedom.

Selling her car had been the right decision, she acknowledged ruefully. She couldn't envisage a time when she would dare drive through this mayhem.

The noise seemed to batter at her eardrums, and the air which reached her through the half-open window was stale and fume-laden.

She turned her gaze resolutely to the shops on either side of the street. She supposed there would come a time when they'd be as familiar to her as those in her own village, but just at the moment it didn't seem likely.

She wanted to ask the cabbie where they were, but her sole remark about the weather had been greeted with a monosyllable, so she stayed silent.

The shops gave way to houses, big and solid, with impressive porticoes and an unmistakable air of affluence.

Olivia felt her throat tighten. It couldn't be far now, she thought, casting an anxious eye at the cab's meter.

Eventually, the taxi turned left into a long curved terrace of tall white houses, each approached by a short flight of stone steps and fronted by railings.

'Did you say number sixteen?' the cabbie called back to her.

'Yes,' she said, dry-mouthed, as they drew to a halt. Leaning forward, she saw smart dark blue paintwork, and a window box still bright with flowers in the September sunlight.

She stood on the pavement, and watched the departing cab as if it was her last link with reality. Then she turned, and looked back at the house. The curtains were half closed, but a ground-floor window was open at the top, and she could hear the faint sound of music.

So Jeremy was at home, she thought, relief flooding over her.

Slowly, she carried her case up the steps. There were two brass bells beside the front door, with one marked 'B'. She pressed the unmarked one, and waited.

For an eternity, nothing happened, and she was just about to ring again when she heard the sound of locks being unfastened inside the house.

She took a deep breath, feeling her mouth shape itself into a nervous rictus of a smile.

The door opened, and Olivia found herself confronted by a complete stranger. Or was he? Although she knew they'd never met, his face seemed oddly familiar just the same.

He was tall, with untidy dark hair falling across his forehead, a beak of a nose, and a shadow of stubble on a determined chin. His eyes were a strange shade between blue and grey that seemed almost silvery, and fringed with long lashes. The deep lines beside his firm-lipped mouth had clearly been scored there by cynical amusement.

Although he wasn't showing much evidence of a sense of humour at the moment. On the contrary, he looked profoundly and wearily irritated.

He was wearing a navy silk dressing gown, which hung open to the waist, revealing a strong, hair-shadowed chest. This garment, which only reached to mid-thigh on his lean, muscular legs, was obviously his only covering, and secured haphazardly by a sash at his waist, Olivia realised with sudden discomfort.

His bored gaze assessed her dismissively, taking in the brief denim skirt, the white shirt and black blazer. Olivia returned his disparaging glance with energy and interest, and saw his mouth tighten.

'Yes?'

Did all Londoners deal in discouraging monosyllables? Olivia wondered.

She lifted her chin. 'I'd like to see Jeremy Attwood, please. He—he's expecting me,' she added, into the ensuing silence.

Leaning against the doorjamb, he gave her another, longer look, which this time took in the suitcase at her feet. The straight dark brows snapped together in a frown.

Then, 'I don't think so,' he said, and made to shut the door.

'Oh, wait.' Dismayed, Olivia lunged forward, grabbing the edge of the door. 'If you'll just tell Jeremy I'm here...'

He shook his head. 'Can't be done. And please let go of my door,' he added coldly. 'You can lose a handful of fingers pulling a stunt like that.'

Olivia disregarded that. 'But he does live here?' And, receiving a brief, affirmative nod, 'Then why won't you fetch him for me?'

'Because he's not here now,' she was told. 'He's away for the weekend, so it's unlikely he was expecting any visitors, least of all you. Now, take your hand away from the door and clear off quietly, like a good girl.'

'Not here?' Olivia repeated, stunned. 'Oh, I don't believe it.'

The silvery eyes became chips of ice. 'Well, I don't propose to allow you to search the house, Miss—er?'

'I'm Olivia Butler. Has Jeremy not mentioned me?'

Slowly and silently he shook his head, his eyes narrowing.

It was a setback, but not irretrievable, she told herself.

She took another deep breath, forcing a smile. 'Well, it doesn't really matter. I—I'm sorry that I've arrived at a bad time, and clearly I should have checked with Jeremy first, but no real harm done.'

'I think,' he said softly, 'that I'll be the judge of that. What exactly do you want, Miss Butler?'

'Firstly, I'd like to come in,' she said. 'I've been on a hot, stuffy train and I'd like to freshen up.'

'Naturally,' he said. 'But what makes you think this is an appropriate place to do it? Was there no restroom at the station—Euston—Waterloo or whatever?'

'Paddington,' she said. 'Of course there was. But that's not the point.'

'Then what is the point?' He was still blocking the doorway. 'I would really like to know.'

No more beating round the bush, Olivia decided.

She said, 'I've come here to live—to be with Jeremy.'

He didn't appear to move, and there was no visible change in his expression, yet Olivia sensed a new and dangerous tension in the atmosphere. She felt as if he'd taken one menacing stride towards her, and she had to overcome the impulse to take a step backwards.

'That's very enterprising of you,' he drawled, after a long pause. 'Did you know that Jeremy is married?'

'I certainly know that he's separated,' she corrected coolly. 'And, anyway, I think that's our business, not yours.'

'On the contrary, I concern myself with all kinds of things.' He paused again. 'I suggest you give me the address where you'll be staying, and I'll pass it on to Jeremy when he returns. Then, if he wishes to make contact, he can.'

'Address?' Olivia repeated in bewilderment. 'But I'm staying here—to wait for him.'

'No,' he said. 'You're not.'

'I don't understand...'

'It's perfectly simple. You want to move in. I'm telling you it's not going to happen.'

Her lips parted helplessly. 'You mean you're turning me away?'

'Now you're getting there,' he approved sardonically. 'Foolish it may be, but I don't give house room to indigent girls who turn up out of the blue claiming acquaintance with a member of the household.'

'I'm far from indigent, and it's rather more than acquaintance,' she said hotly.

'So you say.' He shrugged, and the dressing gown slipped a fraction. 'Sorry, darling. Better luck elsewhere.'

'But I've nowhere else to go.' Olivia heard and despised the faint squeak of panic in her voice. 'I—I don't know anyone in London.'

'Then here's some excellent advice.' His voice was suddenly harsh. 'Go back to wherever you came from, and we'll pretend this never happened.'

The momentary fear gave way to anger. 'I don't need your advice,' she said curtly. 'Nor am I leaving. And when I see Jeremy I'll tell him exactly the kind of welcome I received at his home. You can count on that.'

'Whereas you, sweetheart, can't count on a thing.' She felt her anger matched by his. 'It's a pity you didn't check he'd be around before you set out. Not that it would have made any real difference,' he added, with another perilous shrug. 'I still wouldn't let you stay. Now run along.'

'Damn you,' she said furiously. 'Who the hell do you think you are? And just what right have you to tell me what to do?'

'I happen to own this house.' His voice was like ice. 'Which gives me any rights I choose to assume, lady.'

'But Jeremy...'

'Jeremy is my guest—my temporary lodger, nothing more. Whatever he may have told you, or you chose to believe,' he added with crushing emphasis.

She wanted to scream at him—call him a liar. But there was something about his words which held the ring of truth.

She also wanted to die. But not, she decided, before she had murdered this sneering man in front of her. Until she had hurt and humiliated him, and ground him into the dust before dancing on his unmarked grave.

But that, unfortunately, had to be in the long term. Right now she needed somewhere affordable to stay.

She wasn't poor by any means, she reminded herself. She had a respectable balance in her current account, and a credit card. She could get by until she found a job.

And she'd intended to pay her way with Jeremy. That went without saying. It was going to be a partnership, not charity.

But common sense told her that her resources would soon dwindle if she had to fork out for a London hotel, even for a couple of nights. Nor had she the least idea where to start looking. Anything in this vicinity would be right out of her range.

She looked at the case beside her, and groaned inwardly. How far could she carry it before her arm came out of its socket?

In her home village, she thought, swallowing, they wouldn't treat a stray dog like this.

She looked stonily at her persecutor. 'I don't suppose you'd let me leave my luggage here while I go and look for a room?'

'Quite correct,' he said. 'I wouldn't. And for two pins I'd let you tramp the streets to teach you a much-needed lesson. But I can't do that, because London is not a place where you turn up on the off-chance. You could end up in all kinds of trouble—things you've never envisaged in your worst nightmares. And I don't want that on my conscience.'

'Thanks for the pious platitudes,' Olivia said. She was shaking inwardly with rage. 'What have you in mind? The coal shed?'

'Alas, no.' He reached forward and picked up her case, handling it easily. 'You'd better come in while I talk to someone.'

'You mean I'm being allowed to pollute your sacred portals?' She followed him into a wide hall. On the left, a flight of stairs carpeted in pale green led to the upper floors. On the right, an open door showed her a room fitted out as an office, with a fax machine, a photocopier and a state-of-the-art computer sitting on a workman-like desk. This was where the music was coming from, too.

'Not for long,' he tossed back over his shoulder, leading the way to the rear of the house. 'And don't consider going for squatters' rights, either.'

She'd been about to ask what computer system he used, attempt to establish that she had a life and a career, and wasn't just some helpless hopeful. Now all she hoped was that the whole thing would crash spectacularly at some crucial moment.

He stood back, allowing her to precede him. 'You can wait in here. Please don't make yourself too comfortable. I'm just going to make a phone call.'

'And put some clothes on as well?' Olivia gave the dressing gown an acid glance.

'This,' he said softly, 'is my Saturday morning. I will dress—and do—as I like.' He tightened the sash with ostentatious care. 'Just remember, lady, you came knocking on my door, not the other way round.'

Biting her lip, Olivia walked past him. She found herself in a long rectangular room with one wall that seemed to be made entirely of glass. The main item of furniture was a long refectory table supplied with high-backed oak chairs. On the table, beside a newspaper folded open at an inside page, was a used plate and knife, an empty mug, and a dish of dark red jam. A lingering fragrance of coffee and warm croissant still hung in the air from the adjoining kitchen.

Despite her best efforts, Olivia felt her nose twitch longingly. It had been a long time since the blueberry muffin and carton of hot chocolate which she'd consumed at Bristol Temple Meads Station.

But something warned her that it would be an even longer time before the Owner offered her a sip of his espresso.

Swine, she thought. Greedy, selfish pig.

To take her mind off her empty stomach, she wandered

over to the French windows. Beyond them, she saw a mass of greenery. No walls or fences, she noted, puzzled. Just a riot of tall shrubs and huge trees, already heavy with approaching autumn. There were late-flowering roses, too, and great banks of fuchsias and hydrangeas. Behind the leafy barrier she caught a glimpse of the more strident green of a lawn. And a sunlit dazzle of water.

She drew a swift breath of sheer appreciation. This garden seemed to stretch for ever, its only confine the wide gravelled path which circled it.

It was the last thing she'd expected to find, here in the middle of the city—this wonderful secret wilderness.

It was like the garden behind her parents' home, she thought, although on a vastly larger scale, and for a moment she was assailed by a pang of homesickness so strong that she could have cried out.

'Is something wrong?' The Owner had joined her, tapping out numbers on a cordless phone. Clearly he didn't miss much.

'I—I was just looking at the garden.' Olivia bit her lip. 'It's beautiful. Who—who does it belong to?'

'Everyone whose house backs on to it,' he returned laconically. 'It's a communal venture.'

Then, into the phone, 'Sasha—sorry to annoy you at the weekend, but do you have any place available in that dosshouse of yours?' The lines beside his mouth deepened in amusement as he studied Olivia's sudden rigidity. 'Yes, just one waif and stray—female—wandering in off the street.'

He laughed. 'No, not feline, although I'd say she had claws.' He listened for a moment, grinning. 'Not a chance, my love. She's definitely not my type, and claims to be spoken for anyway. You can? You're a saint. I'll send her round.'

He switched off the phone. 'Well, that's you fixed up.'

She glared at him. 'It never occurred to you that I'd like to make my own arrangements, I suppose?'

'Frankly, no.' His grin deepened. 'So, what was your

major plan? Camping on my doorstep, looking hopeless and helpless, until Jeremy comes back?' He shook his head. 'You'd lower the tone of the neighbourhood.

'No, you'll be all right with Sasha,' he went on, ignoring her furious gasp. 'Her lodgers seem to be a transient population, so she's usually got a room free.'

'Sasha.' Olivia paused. 'Is she Russian?'

'No.' His face softened momentarily, making him seem almost human. Even attractive. And increasing that vague sense of familiarity. 'Just eccentric.'

He gave her a level look with no amusement at all. 'And she's got a kind heart, so I would take it personally if she was made a fool of in any way. By someone doing a runner, for instance, without paying the rent.'

'She'll be paid.' Olivia stopped trying to work out where she could possibly have seen him before, and reverted effortlessly to simply loathing him again. 'Although I don't expect to be staying there long.'

'Of course not. You'll be waiting for Jeremy to provide a suitable love-nest, no doubt. And maybe he will. Only it won't be under my roof.'

'And what the hell has it to do with you?'

He shrugged, unruffled. 'As I mentioned, he's married. Maybe I have more scruples.'

And, as if on cue, a girl's voice called, 'Declan—Declan, darling, where are you?'

Olivia, glancing toward the hall, could see long bare legs descending the stairs. Up to that moment she'd thought no one could be wearing less than her reluctant host, but she was wrong.

The redhead who now appeared and stood, posing coquettishly, in the doorway was using a peach-coloured towel as an inadequate sarong.

'Darling,' she said, pouting reproachfully. 'I woke up and couldn't find you. It was horrid.' She glanced towards Olivia, her glance hardening fractionally. 'But I didn't realise you were—entertaining.'

Her laugh was slightly metallic. 'If this is your latest, then your taste must be slipping.'

Indignant colour flared in Olivia's face at this piece of gratuitous rudeness, but before she could speak Declan stepped forward.

'Wrong on all counts, Melinda, my sweet. Ms Butler is just a passing acquaintance.' He sent Olivia an edged look. 'And, hopefully, passing out of my life for good very soon. Now go back to bed, and I'll see you presently.'

The girl sent him a radiant smile, the tip of her pink tongue caressing her lower lip. 'Is that a promise?' she asked huskily.

'Trust me.' His voice was low-pitched, intimate. The air in the room seemed suddenly alive—electric.

For a shocked moment, Olivia was aware of a slight frisson—a tingle down her own spine.

The Owner might be loathsome, but he was also undeniably sexy—if you liked that sort of thing. As the redhead falling out of the peach towel obviously did, for she was turning and trailing obediently back upstairs.

Olivia felt oddly desolate, suddenly. But small wonder, she thought. After all, she'd arrived expecting a blissful reunion with Jeremy, leading to a passionate consummation, and instead here she was, an intruder, forced into the role of voyeur in someone else's love-life.

There was a strange silence in the room that she needed to break.

She cleared her throat. 'I gather you don't have any moral scruples about your own conduct?'

'Correct.' His grin was unabashed. 'But I'm not married, and never have been. That makes a difference.' He paused. 'Nor am I a home-wrecker.'

The atmosphere tingled again.

Olivia said coldly and clearly, 'If you'll give me this woman's address, I'll go.'

He picked up a message pad and wrote on it. 'It's on the other side of the garden. You'll be able to pick up a black cab at the end of the road if you can't walk that far with your luggage.'

'I hope you don't expect me to thank you effusively.' Olivia accepted the slip of paper, then stalked into the hall and picked up her case.

'I gave up believing in miracles a long time ago.' He unfastened the front door and held it open for her. 'Goodbye, Ms Butler.'

'Oh, that's such a final word,' she said with saccharine sweetness. 'I much prefer *au revoir*, don't you?'

'Not,' he said, 'where you're concerned. I'll tell Jeremy where he can find you. Against my better judgement, I may say,' he added grimly.

The door slammed, shutting her out into a sunlit day which seemed suddenly to have lost its warmth.

'To hell with him,' she muttered, hefting her case down the steps. 'Jeremy will be back soon—and then our life together will begin.'

She gave a last look back at the house.

'And there isn't a thing you can do about it,' she added defiantly, just as if he was listening.

She walked away, without looking back, but found herself wondering, at the same time, if he was standing at one of the windows, watching her go. And, if so, precisely why should it matter to her anyway?

CHAPTER TWO

BROODINGLY, Declan stood at the study window, watching Olivia's slim figure walk away. He was already regretting the quixotic impulse to suggest Sasha as a temporary refuge for her.

I should have taken her to Paddington—put her on the next train west. Saved a hell of a lot of trouble all round, he told himself irritably.

He saw her stop and put down her case, flexing her fingers before transferring it to her other hand and walking on. Her straight back looked gallant, and somehow vulnerable, and he cursed silently. He knew that if he'd been dressed he'd have felt obliged to go after her. Help her with the bloody thing. Take her to Sasha's and introduce her, even.

And yet there was no obligation on his side. On the contrary, he reminded himself bitterly. All he'd probably done by his intervention was make a bad situation worse.

For a moment or two he let his thoughts dwell unpleasantly on Jeremy Attwood, and the things he would have to say to him on his return.

That done, the ball would be in Jeremy's court. This is his damned mess. Let him sort it out, he told himself curtly as he turned determinedly away from the window.

In the meantime, he had a problem of his own to deal with.

He went swiftly up the stairs to the first floor. The drawing room was there, with its panoramic view over the garden, but he didn't waste a glance on it, heading instead for the door at the back of the room which led to his private suite. For his next task he needed to be fully dressed, with his head firmly together.

He stepped through into the narrow passage, and turned right into his dressing room, grabbing some underwear, a white cotton shirt and a pair of jeans. He was on his way into the bathroom opposite when he realised that his bedroom door at the end of the passage was standing ajar, and he knew he'd left it closed.

Still holding his armful of clothing, he moved noiselessly along the passage, his foot tangling in something lying on the floor in front of the door. Mouth tightening, he recognised the peach towel from the guest bathroom on the second floor, and swore under his breath.

He pushed the door wide, and stood in the doorway. Melinda was propped artistically against the pillows of his bed, the covers draped across her hips.

'Hello, darling.' Her smile was pure invitation. 'What an age you've been. Did you manage to get rid of the little brown mouse?'

Declan leaned a shoulder against the doorpost. He felt unutterably weary. 'What are you doing, Melinda?'

'Waiting for you, darling, what else? You did tell me to.'

'No.' He shook his head. 'I said I'd see you later. Not the same thing at all.'

'Don't be picky, sweetie.' She moved slowly, luxuriously, stretching her arms above her head. 'Doesn't this bring back some happy memories?'

'I won't deny that.' Declan kept his eyes fixed steadily on her face. 'But I also remember that you're engaged—to Bill Fenner. Maybe you should, too.'

'Bill's in Warwickshire, staying with his dreary family,' she said with a touch of impatience. 'That's why he didn't take me to the party last night. He can be so boring sometimes.'

'And this is pay-back time—for being boring?' Declan sighed. 'No, Melinda. That's not how it works. Now go and get dressed, and I'll call a cab for you.'

She lifted a hand, admiring the sparkle of the enormous diamond she wore on her left hand.

'Of course,' she said, 'Bill might want to know why I ended up naked in your bed last night. He might feel you'd taken advantage.'

'You actually ended up naked in the spare room bed,' Declan said dispassionately. 'I had to bring you here because you were drunk, and making a nuisance of yourself at the party. I'd have taken you home, but the cab driver refused to go any further in case you threw up. I undressed you for the same reason.' He gave her a level look. 'And Bill will almost certainly *not* want to hear about that.'

'My word, haven't we got virtuous all of a sudden?' Melinda wasn't smiling any more. 'Could this be the influence of Little Miss Well-Scrubbed downstairs?'

'No,' Declan said wearily. 'It's all my own idea. What we had is over now. We've both moved on, so let's leave it like that.'

She threw back the covers and walked towards him, body moving sinuously. 'I could make you change your mind.'

Once, he thought. But not any more. Once he'd have damned all thought of decency, and reached for her. But his mind had stopped wanting her a long time before his body did. A realisation that made him ashamed, because in those last weeks they'd spent together he knew he'd just been using her.

He said more gently. 'You could probably bring a stone statue to life, Melinda. You're a beautiful woman. But you're not my woman—and that makes all the difference.'

'Or perhaps you're just losing it,' she said contemptuously as she went past him. 'And I'll get my own cab,' she threw back over her shoulder.

Maybe she was right, Declan told himself with wry derision as he stood under the shower a short while later. Certainly he hadn't put himself out to find female company lately. And the few dates he'd had had been strictly casual.

He could say he'd been working too hard to pursue any personal relationships. As well as writing a weekly political column for the *Sunday Clarion*, his television commitments were burgeoning. A new series of *Division Bell* was starting next week on First City TV, and he'd also been asked to research and draw up a proposal for a series on Prime Ministers of the past, covering the eighteenth and nineteenth centuries.

Never a dull moment, he thought drily. But it left him with little free time. And what there was he preferred to spend in Ireland, at his parents' stud farm, helping out with the horses rather than doing the social rounds.

However, there'd been a girl at the party last night who'd made her interest in him perfectly clear—until Melinda had started behaving badly, and their hostess had quietly begged him to remove her.

She was an interior decorator, tall, blonde, and definitely attractive, and he had one of her cards somewhere—probably in his jacket.

'In case you want advice about a room,' she'd told him, smiling.

He'd ring her presently, he decided as he towelled himself down. Apologise for his abrupt departure, and ask if she'd like to have dinner. See where it might lead.

She was called Claudia, he remembered, and it was a name he liked. An unusual name—rather like Olivia.

His mouth tightened in irritation. He hadn't planned to throw another thought in her direction. But the image of that slight, lonely figure walking down the road with her case seemed etched on his mind.

All the more reason to call Claudia, he told himself cynically. Because Olivia was bad news, and he wasn't going to waste another thought on her—or any of Jeremy's leavings for that matter.

Sasha was a small woman, slender to the point of emaciation, and draped in a black caftan ornamented with embroidered tropical flowers. She had rich magenta hair which she wore twisted into dozens of little spiral curls, and amazing dark blue eyes, heavily emphasised with kohl. In one hand she held a cheroot. The other was attempting to control a small, brown terrier, spitting out fire and fury on a high-pitched note between a yap and a warble.

Her voice was surprisingly deep and husky, probably, Olivia thought, because of the cheroots.

'So you're Declan's waif.' Olivia was looked up and down, and assessed in one sweeping glance.

'The flat's down here, darling.' She led Olivia down a flight of outside steps to the basement. 'There's only one room, but it has its own separate kitchen, and I had the bathroom fitted two years ago. The rest of the basement I use for storage.'

She opened the living room door, and motioned Olivia to go in. 'The sofa turns into a bed, and I can lend you linen and stuff till you get fixed up. Will it do?'

'It's wonderful,' Olivia admitted. She bit her lip. 'But I must warn you I don't expect to be staying long.'

'People don't.' Sasha shrugged. 'They come and go, and that's fine with me. I'm just a stepping post on their journey.' She paused. 'What about the rent, darling?' The dark blue eyes flicked shrewdly over her again, and she nodded. 'It's seventy-five pounds a week. Can you manage it? You're not working, are you?'

'Not yet,' Olivia said quietly. 'But first thing on Monday morning I'm going to start job-hunting.'

'What sort of thing are you looking for—acting—modelling?'

'Heavens, no.' Olivia felt emotionally battered by the events of the morning, but she managed a weak giggle. 'In Bristol I taught computer systems in offices, but I thought I'd look for a secretarial agency—start by temping.'

'Oh.' Sasha gave her an astonished look. 'You mean real work. Such a novelty. My tenants are usually waiting tables and stacking shelves while they wait to be discovered.'

She swept to the door, the tropical flowers billowing, the dog firmly tucked under her arm. 'When you've unpacked, come on up and we'll have some coffee, introduce ourselves properly. I can brief you on local shops, house rules and things at the same time. Humph and I will be in the kitchen. Just push the door open and yell.'

'Thank you.' Olivia gave her a resolute smile. 'You're very kind.'

'Ah, well, darling,' said Sasha. 'Declan sent you. And I'd do anything for Declan.'

So would I, Olivia thought bitterly, as she unfastened her case. As long as it involved red-hot irons and a few gallons of boiling oil.

But she seemed to have fallen on her feet, she admitted, looking round her. The room was large, the furniture was simple and comfortable, and it was spotlessly clean. And amazingly cheap, for London, too. She'd expected to be charged twice or three times as much.

Sasha's kitchen was big, cosy and chaotic. As she went in Olivia was greeted by the small brown dog, warbling menacingly at full throttle.

'Quiet, Humph, you fool.' Sasha, percolator in hand, swept a pile of newspapers, empty envelopes and special offer coupons from the large pine table to the floor with one magnificent gesture. 'You've got to tell friend from foe. He's a Norfolk terrier with the soul of a Rottweiler,' she added. 'Grab a chair, darling, but not the one with the embroidered cushion—that's Humph's.'

She poured the coffee into attractive pottery mugs, set cream and sugar beside them, and offered home-made carrot cake which Olivia fell on thankfully.

'So, tell me all about yourself,' Sasha said, lighting another cheroot. 'How long have you known my lovely Declan?'

Olivia put down her mug, her stomach churning in swift apprehension. 'Er—not long.'

Oh, come on, she chided herself. Tell the truth, even if

she dumps you back on the pavement. She cleared her throat. 'Actually, I met him for the first time about an hour ago. I—I was looking for someone else entirely.'

'Serendipity,' Sasha nodded, apparently unfazed. 'A happy accident.'

'Not,' Olivia said tautly, 'how I'd have described it.'

'Ah, you clashed.' Sasha gave a throaty chuckle. 'Excellent.'

'I don't think he sees it that way,' Olivia said thinly.

'Well, of course not. He's had to beat women off with sticks since he could walk. And now he's a media personality I expect he gets targeted by all sorts.'

'Media personality?' Olivia stared at her, while connections in her brain jangled into place. 'My God,' she said in a hollow voice. 'I've just realised—he's Declan Malone. He interviews politicians on television. I knew I'd seen him somewhere.'

But not, she thought, next to naked on a doorstep.

Sasha gurgled. 'You could say that, darling. I think I'm going to like you.' She paused, frowning slightly. 'Declan can be abrasive sometimes, because his work demands it, but his heart's in the right place or you wouldn't be here now. Why, he's even got one of his in-laws lodging with him, which I think is carrying charity too far.'

Olivia swallowed her last morsel of carrot cake. 'One of his in-laws?' she repeated.

'Well, almost.' Sasha gestured broadly, doing no good to yet another pile of miscellaneous paperwork. 'The chap who's married to his cousin Maria. But she and Declan were practically brought up as brother and sister, so I suppose it counts.'

'Yes,' Olivia said, dry-mouthed. 'I—suppose it does.'

She felt deathly cold—shrivelling inside. She wanted to throw her head back and howl like a banshee.

My God, she thought, despairingly. He's Maria's cousin, and I just marched up to his door and laid my claim to her husband. What have I said? What have I done?

Oh, Jeremy—*Jeremy*. Why didn't you warn me?

Because he didn't know you were about to descend on him, a small, flat voice in her head reminded her. You did it all off your own bat, and now you have to live with the consequences. Whatever they are.

'Are you all right?' Sasha was staring at her. 'You look as if you've seen a ghost, darling.'

'No.' Olivia mustered a smile. 'I think I've just realised how much I've bitten off—and I'm wondering if I can chew it.'

'While on the subject of chewing.' Sasha grabbed an envelope and drew a swift sketch map on the back of it. 'The Portobello Road, darling, and our closest food source. Today's market day, so you'll find everything you need, but keep a close grip on your wallet. Pickpockets are practically endemic down there, so try not to look like a tourist.'

She didn't feel like a tourist, Olivia thought an hour later, as she picked her way warily along the crowded Portobello pavements. More like an alien from the Planet Zog.

She'd spent a fraught hour with Sasha, being interrogated with the utmost charm on her background from birth to the present day. Nothing to hide there, but she'd had to dance round the subject of why she'd come to London, and how she'd happened to fetch up in W11.

She'd said far too much about her association with Jeremy already, and she suspected Sasha would approve no more than Declan Malone.

She'd been quite glad to make her urgent need to shop for provisions an excuse to escape.

And now here she was, walking down the Portobello Road. At first she thought she'd come to the wrong place, because all she could see on both sides of the road were antiques shops. The displays of silver and crystal were certainly mouth-watering, but there was no sign of any food outlets.

She crossed a road, and suddenly found herself absorbed into an alternative reality. A rowdy, brash reality, where dozens of ethnic accents brayed and clashed. Where clumps of street musicians vied for attention with a non-stop assault on the eardrums. Where stall-holders bellowed incomprehensible special offers. Olivia was wearing her bag slung diagonally across her body under her jacket, and she kept a protective hand on it as she found herself almost borne along on a tidal wave of humanity.

She was used to crowds, for heaven's sake. She'd lived and worked in Bristol. But here the noise and numbers suddenly threatened to overwhelm her.

She'd never seen a market like it. As well as all the fruit and vegetables on offer, there were innumerable stalls offering bric-à-brac, second-hand clothing—including a display of old fur coats and military uniforms from another century—books, jewellery and musical instruments.

The temptation to linger and explore was fierce, but buying food had to be her main priority.

She turned and fought her way back, diving into a supermarket with something like relief. She filled a basket with staples, then pushed her way up the road to a specialist bakery she'd noticed earlier, where tempting displays of every kind of bread and pastry were presented outside for customers to pick and mix.

Olivia chose some focaccia bread, with a mini-baguette filled with smoked ham and salad, which, with fruit, would serve as lunch. She selected apples, plums, tomatoes and peppers from a street stall, and then stopped at the old-fashioned butcher's further up the road and bought a chicken and enough minced pork and beef to make a pasta sauce.

On her way back, she passed the end of a cobbled mews and paused for a moment, looking wistfully at the narrow smart houses, painted in pastel colours. One of them she saw, even had a 'For Sale' board hanging from its first-floor balcony.

As she hesitated a couple came out of the house opposite, walking fast, hand in hand, the girl looking up into her companion's face and laughing. Olivia stepped back to let them pass, an intense pang of envy twisting inside her as she wondered what it would be like to live there with someone you loved.

She allowed herself to indulge a brief fantasy of being there with Jeremy. Wandering out to buy fresh croissants and oranges to squeeze for breakfast, while he stayed in bed with the newspapers. Then, later, going for a stroll together round the second-hand bookshops and junk stalls, choosing something for the house—a piece of pottery, maybe, or some glassware. Something to provide memories in the years ahead.

She stopped herself right there. At the moment there was no guarantee that she was going to share any time with Jeremy, she thought wretchedly. Not after her appalling gaffe at Lancey Gardens.

She shuddered as she walked slowly back up the hill, weighed down by her shopping and the remembrance of the morning's confrontation.

Because she could just imagine the row there would be when Jeremy got back, she thought despondently.

Declan Malone had caught her off guard—flicked her on the raw—but that was no excuse. She'd behaved like an idiot, pushing herself forward like that before she'd sussed out the situation.

If only Jeremy had told her that he was holed up temporarily with his wife's cousin. Instead, she'd gained the opposite impression—that he had his own independent flat, that he was making a life which she would be able to share.

I couldn't have been listening properly, she admitted, with a sigh. Or else I simply heard what I wanted to hear.

Nothing, but nothing was working out as she'd expected. And she could well end up on her own in one of the world's great uncaring capitals.

Or she could go back to Bristol, she reminded herself. No one apart from Beth knew why she'd come to London, and her flatmate was too kind and loyal to have spread the word. She could probably even get her old job back.

My God, she thought in swift horror, as she crossed the road to Lancey Terrace. That was real defeatist talk. Return to square one and occupy her familiar rut. When in fact it had been more than time for a change. For her to take hold of her life by the scruff of its neck and shake it.

She had a career—valuable job skills to offer. She could earn her living—pay her way. She'd come to London to share Jeremy's life, not to become some pathetic dependent.

And whatever happened, she intended to survive.

Lifting her chin, she strode the last hundred yards.

Her shopping unpacked and put away, Olivia sat down to eat her lunch and take a long look round her. The flat was starting to look occupied, and she had her small portable radio to fill the silence. She'd noticed, too, there was a TV aerial in the room. And from the information that Sasha had thrown at her earlier about Notting Hill Gate she reckoned she'd be able to rent a set quite easily.

That will be my project for the afternoon, she thought. Keep busy—keep interested—and, above all, don't brood.

She'd found a vase in one of the cupboards. She'd get some flowers to go in it. And some wine. If it turned out there was nothing to celebrate, then she'd drown her sorrows instead, she decided, squaring her shoulders.

She got out her *A to Z* of London, working out the shortest route to the Gate.

Sasha had told her she could find anything there, and that seemed to be true, she thought as she battled with the other Saturday afternoon shoppers. Like Portobello, it seemed to be fizzing with life. She gave herself time to look properly, lingering in front of boutiques and reading the menus of the various bistros, walking, inevitably, much further than she'd planned.

But if Notting Hill was to be her home, at least for the

time being, she needed to get to know it. She wanted to look as confident and purposeful as the people who streamed past her, and feel it too.

She thought suddenly, I want to belong.

At a wine shop she bought some red Italian wine to go with the pasta, a decent Chardonnay for the chicken, and an optimistic Bollinger for her reunion with Jeremy, investing in a strong canvas bag in which to lug her purchases home, as most of her shopping was likely to be done on the hoof from now on.

She discovered a TV store without difficulty, and ended up buying a reconditioned portable with a reasonable warranty for far less than the cost of an annual rental, treating herself to a cab to get it back to Lancey Terrace. After all, she reminded herself, she couldn't waste good job-hunting time waiting at the flat for a delivery to be made.

In spite of her personal reservations, there was a curious satisfaction in making her basement look like home.

But, when it came to it, the idea of spending her first evening in London concocting a pasta sauce for one held little appeal.

Up to now there'd always been people around her—family first, then friends, and flatmates. Always someone to laugh with, or moan to, or simply exchange the news of the day.

This was her first experience of being single in the city, and she needed to tackle it positively.

So she wouldn't skulk in the flat, feeling hard done to. She would go out. Go to the cinema in the Gate, and have a meal afterwards. Make her first night in London an occasion.

She changed, putting on black leggings, a cream shirt, and a long black linen jacket, and set off. She had a choice of films, including a well-reviewed romantic comedy, but it seemed safer in her present state of mind to opt for a thriller, with a plot convoluted enough to keep her mind engaged, and, consequently, off her personal problems.

She emerged feeling more relaxed then she'd done all day. Now all that remained was to find somewhere to eat. Probably not easy, she realised, surveying the still crowded pavements. Maybe she'd have to settle for a take-away.

She'd intended to head for one of the bistros she'd checked out earlier, but instead found herself wandering up Kensington Park Road.

The lit window of a restaurant drew her across the street, but one look was enough to convince her that it was not only full to bursting point with beautiful people, but, more significantly, out of her price range.

She was just moving on when she saw a diner seated at a table for two in the window itself turn, hand raised, to summon a waiter.

She recognised him with stomach-churning immediacy. Declan Malone, she thought, stiffening, her hackles on full alert. But not with the morning's exotic redhead, she noticed at once. His evening's companion was a willowy blonde decorously clad in a dark trouser suit. For the moment anyway. Presumably the peach towel outfit came later.

'Poor girl,' she muttered under her breath. 'Does she realise she's simply feeding the ego of a serial womaniser?'

Clearly she didn't, because she was devouring Declan Malone with her eyes, to the complete detriment of the food on her plate. And he was looking at her and smiling in a way that had been totally lacking in his dealings with Olivia.

In fact, Olivia acknowledged without pleasure, she would hardly have recognised him.

A taxi drew up, and three girls got out, all stick-thin, and talking and giggling at the tops of their voices.

As the new arrivals pranced past her into the restaurant, shrieking their hellos and air-kissing everyone within reach, Olivia started, as if she'd been woken abruptly from some spell.

What the hell am I doing? she demanded silently. Hanging round here with my nose pressed against the glass like the Little Match Girl? Do I want him to look up and see me?

Hastily, she turned away, retracing her steps towards the Gate.

She realised with sudden bleakness that her appetite had totally deserted her. And, more disturbingly, that she had never felt quite so cold, or so lonely in her life before.

Claudia Lang was not a particularly conceited girl, but she was sufficiently keyed in to know when her dinner partner's attention was wandering, and human enough to be piqued by it.

She reached across the table and put a scarlet-tipped hand on Declan's sleeve.

'Is something wrong?'

Startled, Declan wrenched his frowning gaze back from the window.

'No—I'm sorry. I—thought I saw someone outside. Someone I knew.'

Claudia directed a sceptical glance over her shoulder at the darkness beyond the window. 'Then you must have X-ray vision,' she commented lightly. 'Do you want to go and check?'

'Of course not.' The frown faded, and the smile he sent her was charming and repentant. 'I'm probably wrong, and anyway, it's really—not important.' He paused, then added with cold emphasis, 'Not important at all.'

And wondered why he'd needed to say that.

CHAPTER THREE

A GOOD night's sleep was all she needed to cheer her up and put her right. That was what Olivia had told herself. But sleep was proving elusive.

The sofa-bed was comfortable enough, but quite apart from the non-stop traffic noise—did no one else ever go to bed?—there was no air in her room. Although she'd opened the window at the top, the atmosphere still felt heavier than the quilt she'd kicked off. The curtains hung unmoving.

The dial on her alarm clock told her it was nearly three in the morning, and so far she hadn't closed her eyes.

I'm just on edge about seeing Jeremy again, she thought. And it's a strange bed, strange room, strange city. What else can I expect but insomnia?

She got up and padded down the narrow passage into the kitchen. She poured milk into a saucepan, and set it on the hob, then opened the tin of drinking chocolate she'd included in her groceries.

Of course, if everything had gone according to plan she wouldn't have been doing much sleeping anyway, she acknowledged, her face warming slightly.

She supposed Jeremy would have taken her to a hotel. Because they certainly wouldn't have been allowed to be together at Lancey Gardens, as Declan Malone had made more than clear.

King of the double standard, she thought stormily, slamming the inoffensive tin of chocolate back in the cupboard. No prizes for guessing how he was spending the night.

Glumly, she poured the hot milk into a beaker, and stirred in the chocolate powder.

One of the things she'd been trying to figure as she stared

35

into the darkness was possible damage limitation, but so far she hadn't come up with a thing.

From Sasha's remarks, it was clear that Declan Malone sincerely cared about Maria, and had little idea that her marriage was in such serious trouble.

Not until I showed up anyway, she thought, pulling a face. Although, if they are so close, it seems odd that she hasn't confided in him.

She sat at the small, round living room table, her hands cupped round the beaker, her mind going wearily over the same ground, and finding naught for her comfort.

She could only hope that Jeremy would see she'd acted in their best interests, and not mind that she'd jumped the gun.

And if Declan threw him out it would give him an incentive to find a place where they could be together, she encouraged herself. Maybe her intervention would be the catalyst that changed things at last.

If only he could be persuaded to look at it that way.

She'd half expected to be awake all night, but almost immediately after she got back into bed she found her thoughts swirling drowsily into emptiness.

Only to discover that she was standing in front of a giant pane of glass, and she could see Jeremy on the other side. She tapped on the glass, and called to him, but he didn't seem to see or hear her, and she knew she had to get to him—to make him listen. She started banging on the glass with both fists until it suddenly disintegrated, parting in front of her, then flowing round her like thick mist.

She began searching through the mist for Jeremy, hands outstretched, crying out his name, and at last felt her wrists taken. Gripped tightly.

But when she looked up, peering through the stifling grey miasma, she saw that the man who held her was not Jeremy, but Declan Malone, his eyes glittering like ice.

'Oh, God.' Olivia sat bolt-upright, her heart hammering. For a moment she was totally disorientated, then she saw

the sun pouring through a gap in the green curtains and
realised she'd been dreaming.

A glance at her alarm clock confirmed that she'd slept
late too.

Her head felt heavy and her eyes were full of sand, so
that it would have been very easy to lie back and sleep
again. Fatally easy.

'Just asking for more nightmares,' she muttered, pushing
back the quilt and swinging her feet to the floor. 'And who
needs them?'

She set coffee to brew, and poured orange juice into a
glass, then went to shower and dress.

By the time she'd drunk her coffee, and eaten two slices
of toast and marmalade, she was beginning to feel marginally human again.

She washed her few dishes, then tidied the bed into a
sofa again, tucking the bedding away inside as Sasha had
shown her.

And now, she thought, I have the rest of the day in front
of me. What shall I do with it?

Not that she could do very much, she reminded herself.
She needed to stay round the flat so that Jeremy could contact her there. But she could at least walk to the Gate and
get the Sunday papers. Fill the time that way, because, a
small, sober voice in her head suggested, she could be in
for a long wait.

If she'd thought the streets would be quieter on Sunday,
she soon discovered her mistake. But there was a different,
more relaxed atmosphere.

Olivia found a seat at a pavement table outside a café,
and ordered herself a cappuccino while she settled down
for a leisurely bout of people-watching.

It was something she normally enjoyed, but somehow,
today, it only seemed to deepen her sense of isolation.
There were too many couples, strolling hand in hand in the
sunshine, smiling into each other's eyes.

Eventually, she left her coffee unfinished, and walked quietly back to her basement.

I won't always feel like this, she promised herself. I won't always feel an outsider. One day—soon—I'll be walking with Jeremy, and someone will be watching me—envying me. One day...

She tried to visualise it. Fix the image in her mind like a lodestar. But instead, incomprehensibly, she found herself remembering the restaurant last night, and Declan Malone smiling at his companion. And herself outside. Looking in.

For a moment she felt totally frozen, all the muscles in her throat tightening suddenly, as if she was going to cry.

Then her hands clenched fiercely into fists at her side.

Oh, for heaven's sake, she thought in self-derision. Pull yourself together.

She made herself an omelette for lunch, and afterwards, when she'd cleared away, she put some music on, and stretched out on the sofa with the crossword.

She'd barely started when there was a knock at the door, and Sasha called, 'Olivia, may I come in, darling?'

Today, the caftan was emerald-green, and she was carrying Humph tucked under her arm.

'It all looks very nice.' She cast an appraising glance around her. 'Does it feel like home? Not yet, I dare say.'

She seated herself in a swirl on one of the dining chairs. Humph wriggled to get down, then trotted over to the sofa and jumped up beside Olivia, circling twice on his chosen cushion, then settling down with a sigh.

'Ah,' Sasha said with satisfaction. 'You've been given official approval. Isn't that nice?'

Olivia was bound to agree as she stroked the silky golden-brown fur, and found herself observed by a bright dark eye.

'But what I really came for, darling, is this.' Sasha laid a large iron key on the table. 'Now that you're a resident, you have the right to use the garden. This unlocks the main gate.'

'Really?' Olivia's sore heart lifted slightly as she remembered the magical green wilderness she'd spied from Declan's window. 'That's—wonderful.'

'And these are the communal rules.' Sasha put a typewritten sheet beside the key. 'Just look them through when you have a moment. Now I must dash. I have to take Humph for his constitutional before my bridge party, and I'm running late as usual.'

'Couldn't I take him for you later?' Olivia suggested. 'After all, it seems a pity to disturb him when he's so comfortable.'

'I can't ask you to do that,' Sasha objected. 'It's such an imposition…'

'No,' Olivia said firmly. 'I'd enjoy it.' She hesitated. 'I haven't a great deal else to do.'

Sasha gave her a swift, shrewd glance, then nodded briskly. 'Very well, darling. Here's his lead—and also a key to my flat. Just pop him into the kitchen when you bring him back, and then drop the key through the letterbox.'

'Are you sure about this?' Olivia accepted the key, brows raised. 'After all, you hardly know me.'

'Call it instinct. Humph trusts you.' Sasha smiled suddenly, almost mistily. 'And my beloved would have liked you too. Have fun.' And in a whirl of emerald she was gone.

As Olivia returned to her crossword she found herself wondering who Sasha's beloved had been.

She'd finished her puzzle by the time Humph decided he was ready for his walk. He pranced ahead of her up the steps and along the road to a pair of wrought-iron gates, which Olivia used her key to open, then locked behind her.

As soon as she stepped inside, the peace of the place seemed to wrap itself around her. Even the incessant traffic noise faded to a distance.

She began to walk along the gravelled path, glancing shyly around her, half expecting to be challenged.

The fine weather had brought the residents out in force she noticed. They spilled out of their houses and flats on to their rear steps, or the nearby grass, chatting together, playing with their children, drinking wine, picnicking, or attending to the plants in the vast ornamental urns which stood at the back of almost every property. All of them were too occupied to pay her anything but passing attention, although some of them seemed to recognise Humph and gave her a half-smile.

Presently, Humph turned off the main path, choosing a track through the towering shrubs which Olivia guessed was his preferred route.

It was rather like trying to unravel a maze, she thought as he trotted ahead of her, following some scent or other.

'I only hope you know the way back,' she told him.

Eventually she found herself in a massive lawned area with a large central pond. Humph, however, pulled her across it to where a gap in the surrounding shrubbery was marked by an ornamental arch, decorated with climbing roses.

A narrow path led to a small clearing—a patch of grass with a sundial at its centre, and one elderly wooden seat. Very sheltered, and very peaceful, Olivia thought approvingly.

She walked across to the sundial, and read the inscription. *'Love makes Time pass. Time makes Love pass.'* Now there's a cynical viewpoint, she thought, wandering back to the seat and subsiding on to its aged timbers.

Humph was getting restive, so she bent down and slipped off his leash.

'Don't wander off,' she adjured him. And saw, as she straightened, a movement in the bushes. A cat.

She grabbed at Humph's collar. But in a crescendo of yapping he was off, his legs a blur, pursuing the fleeing cat through the shrubs with Olivia flying after the pair of them.

She hurled herself through the bushes, guided by another flurry of hysterical barking and an angry feline yowl, and arrived panting on the gravelled walk, just in time to see Humph's hindquarters disappearing up a flight of stone steps and in through some open French windows.

'Oh, no,' she groaned, and started after him.

She was halfway up when Declan Malone appeared at the window. He was carrying Humph, who was licking his face frantically.

He looked at Olivia, his mouth tightening inimically.

'Miss Butler,' he said expressionlessly. 'Now why am I not surprised? If you're here looking for Jeremy, he's not back yet.'

'I'm not,' Olivia said stiffly, silently cursing the day she was born.

He was wearing chinos, she noticed, and a white shirt, with the sleeves turned back to reveal tanned forearms, and his feet were bare. His hair was damp, as if he'd just got out of the shower, and she found herself wondering if last night's lady was still around somewhere.

Not, she reminded herself hastily, that it had anything to do with her.

She mounted the last few steps and took the little dog from him. 'I didn't mean to disturb you. Humph was chasing a cat. I—just followed him through the bushes.'

'You seem to have brought a fair bit of them with you.' Declan reached out and removed a twig and some leaves from her hair. It was the last thing she'd expected him to do, and an odd shiver ran through her at his touch.

He said abruptly, 'The rules of the garden state that dogs must be kept on leads at all times. Did Sasha not tell you?'

Olivia bit her lip, recalling the typewritten sheet she hadn't bothered to read. 'Yes—I mean, I think so.'

He said silkily, 'But then rules don't mean much to you, do they, Miss Butler?'

'And you seem to invent yours as you go along, Mr Malone,' she returned icily. 'But I'll make sure I remember in the future.'

'You do that,' he said with a certain grimness.

'Before I go,' she said, 'there's something I'd like to say. You implied I was a home-wrecker. But it's not true. Jeremy's marriage was finished long before I met him again.'

'You've known him for a while?'

'It seems like all my life. Perhaps like you—and Maria.'

'I doubt that.'

She said, 'Sasha told me she was your cousin—that you were close. So you must have known that things were—going wrong.'

'I've never had many illusions about the state of her marriage.' His tone was short. 'But that doesn't mean I'd choose to connive at its breakdown.'

'Nor I.' Olivia lifted her chin. 'But—these things happen.'

'Indeed they do,' he drawled. 'I've read the statistics.' He gave her a level look. 'Have you anything else to say in mitigation?'

'No,' she said. 'Actually, I didn't have to explain to you at all. But I felt I owed it to myself.' She paused. 'Do you have no other comment?'

'Nothing you'd particularly want to hear. Just a repetition of advice already given. Which is: go back to—' his brows lifted enquiringly '—where was it?'

'Bristol,' she said stonily. 'And I'm staying here.' She clipped Humph's lead to his collar. 'I'd better take him home.' She hesitated. 'And I apologise for letting him chase the cat. Is it all right?'

'Fighting fit. It was the Fosters' Maximilian.' He put out a hand and scratched the top of the little dog's head. 'If he ever turned on Humph he'd have him on toast. So take care, Miss Butler.'

'Of Humph?' Her voice was saccharine-sweet. 'Of course I will.'

'Of everything,' he said. 'And I'm sure you won't.'

She turned and descended the steps, aware of his eyes

boring into her spine. As she reached the path she looked back at him.

'When Jeremy does come back, will you ask him to call me, please, on my mobile? He has my number.'

His mouth twisted. 'I'll refrain from the cheap retort. And, yes, I'll tell him to make contact—if that's really what you want.'

'Yes,' she said lifting her chin. 'It is.'

He gave her one last cool look, then walked back into the house and closed the French windows behind him.

This, Olivia told an unresponsive pane of glass, is getting to be a habit. But at least this time she'd had the last word. Or had she? With Declan Malone it was difficult to be certain.

But she could ensure it was the last word in another sense, she thought as she walked away, Humph prancing beside her.

She could take immense care never to set eyes on Declan Malone again.

In a city the size of London, it shouldn't be too hard.

And she'd begin by never straying to his side of the garden again, she vowed silently.

Declan was not in a good mood when he returned to his computer screen. Introducing the Butler girl to Sasha had been a bad mistake, he told himself savagely. What the hell had possessed him to do such a thing, instead of sending her away with a flea in her ear? Now she was ensconced just across the garden, and far too close for comfort.

He shook his head in exasperation, glaring at his notes on William Pitt the Younger, which now seemed stilted and totally without interest. Maybe in trying to breathe new life into these long-dead politicians he'd simply bitten off more than he could chew.

Or maybe that damned girl was sitting in his skull, distorting his thinking.

Oh, come on, he derided himself. She's just a passing

irritation, not a major problem. When Jeremy returned, he'd give him a sharp piece of his mind, and tell him to get rid of her or get out. And that would settle the matter.

Declan pressed 'Save' and deliberately switched his thoughts with far more satisfaction to last night's dinner with Claudia.

She was lively, intelligent and extremely attractive, he reflected. And she'd let him know, albeit with charming subtlety, that she was also attracted to him.

Without conceit, he knew that he could probably have ended the evening in her bed. But he'd decided instead to slow the pace. Establish a relationship before taking the quantum leap into intimacy.

They'd talked about music and theatre over their meal. He'd give it a couple of days, then ask her if she'd like to go to the Ibsen revival that had been so well reviewed.

Claudia had admitted to liking cooking, so it was on the cards she'd offer to make dinner for him. And then they'd see...

He frowned swiftly. It all seemed rather measured—even calculating, perhaps—but what the hell? He was past expecting to be knocked flat by passion at first sight—the genuine *coup de foudre* that people sighed about.

On the other hand, he wanted to be sure that when he married his marriage would last, and not fall into the kind of disarray he saw all around him.

Like Maria and Jeremy, he thought grimly, and cursed under his breath as the Butler girl invaded his mind's eye again.

I should have sent her packing, he told himself, restively. So why didn't I? And what can I do to salvage the situation?

He swung his chair round and picked up the phone, punching in a familiar number.

'Maria?' His face relaxed into a smile. 'So, how's it going?'

*   *   *

As evening approached Olivia was on tenterhooks, pacing up and down her room, eyeing her mobile phone. Willing it to ring.

When it finally obliged, she pounced on it with a sob of relief. 'Jeremy?'

'No, it's Beth. Just calling to see how you're settling in?' Beth paused. 'I gather lover boy isn't around?'

'Not at the moment.' Olivia managed to sound amused as well as rueful. 'I would choose a weekend when he's working away. But I'm expecting him back any minute now,' she added hastily.

'Then I won't keep you. I just wanted to make sure you were all right, and check on your address. It is number sixteen, isn't it?'

Olivia hesitated. 'No,' she said reluctantly. 'Actually it's 21B Lancey *Terrace*. As Jeremy wasn't here, I thought it was better to establish my own base. I've found this terrific bedsit. Cheap too. I can't believe how lucky I've been.' She paused, aware of the over-brightness in her tone.

'Well,' Beth said, after a pause of her own, 'just as long as you're OK. Let me know how the job-hunting goes.'

'I will. Bless you.' Olivia switched off the phone and put it down beside her on the sofa, homesickness washing over her like a tidal wave. She'd planned to call her parents, but wasn't sure she could manage it without bursting into tears and worrying them both to death. Better to wait until she had some good news for them, she thought. Something that would lift her own spirits too.

She wasn't used to hiding things from the people she loved, or pretending. She'd let them think that coming to London was a career move. She hadn't told them that her future included Jeremy, because she knew they wouldn't approve while he was still nominally a married man.

She wished she could have confided in Beth. Admitted that nothing was working out as she'd planned. That she felt stranded, and lonelier than she'd ever dreamed.

And threatened, she realised, as an image of Declan

Malone's dark, unsmiling face forced its way into her mind. She'd made an enemy there that she didn't need.

She switched on the television and tried to interest herself in a detective series she usually enjoyed, but the twists and turns of the plot couldn't hold her attention tonight.

It was midnight when she finally came to terms with the certainty that Jeremy was not going to telephone after all.

And it was another hour before she eventually cried herself to sleep.

She felt tired and jaded the next morning, which wasn't how she needed to present herself at all, she thought, giving herself a mental kick. She was looking for a job, and she wanted to impress.

She dressed with extra care, choosing a dark grey suit with a faint pinstripe, a white shirt, and black pumps with a medium heel.

She would settle for temporary work to ease her immediate cash-flow situation, she'd decided, but she also planned to register with a couple of recruitment agencies. Try and capitalise on her computer skills.

Perhaps, when she and Jeremy were living together and settled, she'd freelance, working from home, she told herself, determined to be positive about their relationship.

After all, there could be a dozen reasons why he hadn't rung her last night. And she wasn't going to allow herself any more doubts, or fits of the blues.

But if she'd hoped to walk straight into the perfect job, she was disappointed. The first temp bureau she visited had a full quota already, she was told, and the second could only offer part-time work at rates that wouldn't even pay the rent, let alone feed her.

She was climbing the stairs to a third place when her phone rang.

'Livvy?' Jeremy asked. 'Darling, what on earth are you doing here? I could hardly believe my ears when I got your message.'

Olivia leaned against the wall, aware of a small, painful knot in her chest.

She said, 'Aren't you pleased?'

'I'm delighted, naturally,' he said quickly. 'But a bit stunned too. I mean, we didn't actually discuss this—did we?'

'Maybe I felt it was time for action rather than words.' There was a crack in the plaster beside her. It looked like the shape of a pregnant woman, she thought, tracing it with her finger. She said, 'When am I going to see you?'

'Well—tonight, obviously.' He paused. 'How about we meet for a drink when I finish work.'

'A drink?' she echoed, trying to fight down her instinctive dismay. 'But, Jeremy, we need to talk—make some plans.'

'Of course we do, and we will.' He sounded brisk. 'But I'm a bit pushed at the moment. Now, there's a bar near Liverpool Street Station called Dirty Dick's. I'll see you there at five-thirty. Bless you, sweetheart. Must dash.'

Olivia switched off her phone and replaced it in her bag. It wasn't the reaction she'd been expecting, she thought flatly, but at least he wasn't angry about her gaffe at Declan's. And in a few hours she was going to see him.

She straightened her shoulders and continued her way up the stairs.

Just hearing Jeremy's voice on the phone seemed to have changed her luck, because the woman who interviewed her this time seemed friendly and upbeat about Olivia's chances of finding work.

'However, it won't necessarily be in this area,' she said. 'We have several branches, and clients all over London, and we deal with everything from large multinationals down to one-man bands. Do you drive?'

'Yes, but I don't have a car. Travelling doesn't worry me, though,' she said, mentally crossing her fingers.

'And you've no ties? No children to be picked up from school?'

'I'm not married.'

The other woman raised her eyebrows. 'What difference does that make these days?' She handed Olivia an application form. 'Complete these details for me, please, including a daytime telephone number where you can be contacted, and I'll have a placement for you by the end of the week—or earlier, maybe, if someone calls in sick.' She produced another form. 'And these are the agency's terms and conditions of employment. Read them through, and sign at the bottom if you're satisfied.' She paused, and smiled. 'My name's Sandra Wilton. Welcome to Service Group.'

Olivia allowed herself a modest lunchtime celebration of a hot chicken sandwich and a diet drink, then set out to unravel the mysteries of the London Underground system.

By the end of the day she was confident enough to launch herself towards the City on the Central Line.

She found Dirty Dick's quite easily, hesitating for a moment over whether to choose the door straight ahead of her or go downstairs. She opted for street level, pausing just inside the door so that her eyes could readjust to the subdued lighting. It was a big room, with a long bar, a wooden floor, and barrels for tables.

It was already filling up noisily with dark City suits and briefcases, and Olivia paused, staring around her, trying to locate Jeremy.

She saw him at last, waving at her from the side of the room, where a shelf had been built along the wall, and equipped with stools for customers who preferred to sit.

Her heart leapt as she threaded her way through the laughing, chattering groups, but she couldn't help wishing that he'd come to her.

'Darling.' His arms closed round her, hugging her tightly against him. 'This is amazing. God, it's so good to see you. I've missed you so much.'

'I've missed you too.' Now that the moment of truth had come, she felt oddly shy. 'That's why I came.'

'My love.' His eyes caressed her. 'I wish this wasn't such a public place.' His smile was intimate—warming. He paused. 'I ordered dry white wine for you. I hope that's all right.' He handed her a glass, then raised his own. 'And there's only one possible toast. To us.'

'To us,' she echoed, filling her eyes with him. He was wearing an immaculate dark blue suit, and his hair had been cut shorter than she'd seen it before. Almost severe. And, she thought fondly, he'd put on a little weight. But she wouldn't tell him that.

'So,' he said. 'Where are you staying and how long are you going to be here?'

'How long?' Olivia repeated uncomprehendingly.

'Well, yes, sweetheart. Have you got a week—two weeks?'

The wine tasted sharp suddenly, leaving bitterness in her throat.

She tried to laugh. 'Jeremy—I'm here for good. I—I thought you realised that.' She took a deep breath. 'I've got a bedsit, and I'm looking for a job.' She paused. 'Didn't Declan Malone tell you?'

'No, of course not. He just said you'd been to the house, asking for me,' Jeremy said slowly. 'Livvy, let me get this straight. You're telling me you've thrown up everything in Bristol and moved here? Without a word to me first?'

'I thought you'd be pleased.' Her voice faltered slightly. 'After all, it's what we always intended.'

'Yes, I know.' His voice held a touch of impatience. 'But not at this particular moment in time. It could cause—problems.'

Olivia stiffened slightly. 'With Declan?'

'He's certainly part of it.' He grimaced. 'Thank God you were discreet when you went to the house.'

'What do you mean?' Olivia asked uneasily.

'I mean letting him think that we're old acquaintances from Bristol days, and you simply came round to look me up while you were in town.'

She thought in bewilderment, But I didn't—and he doesn't. What's going on? What game is Declan playing?

She said quietly, 'Would it be so terrible if he knew the truth?'

'It could be disastrous.' Jeremy frowned. 'Listen, darling, I want a no-blame, no-hassle divorce, with a clean-break settlement. That's essential, believe me. If Maria found out about you—if Declan told her…'

His frown deepened. 'Well, she's a hotshot lawyer. Need I say more? She could string the whole thing out until doomsday—find all kinds of sticks to beat me with.' He gave her an intense look. 'Do you understand what I'm saying?'

'I think so.' Olivia put her glass down on the shelf. Now, if ever, was the time to confess that their secret was already blown, she realised unhappily. But she already knew that she couldn't risk Jeremy's anger. That she wasn't going to say a thing.

She said, 'So, you want me to keep up the pretence—maintain a low profile?'

He nodded. 'Just for a time, my sweet. While I'm still living with Declan. You must see that I have to tread carefully.'

'Wouldn't it be better to find a place of your own?'

'Of course it would. And I am flat-hunting. But it's not that simple. I need something in absolutely the right area.' He paused. 'Where are you living, by the way?'

'Not far from you. I'm in Lancey Terrace with someone called Sasha.'

'That old witch,' Jeremy said disagreeably. 'How did you find her?'

She bit her lip. 'It was Declan. I—mentioned I needed somewhere to stay—temporarily.'

'Quite the bloody philanthropist, isn't he?' Jeremy gave a short laugh. 'Well, it's done now, I suppose. But it's going to make it damned difficult for us to see each other on our own. If I come visiting, Sasha's bound to see me and report to Declan.' He sighed irritably. 'If you'd just told me what you were planning, I could have found you a place well away from W11.'

'But absolutely the right area?' Olivia asked drily.

Jeremy flushed slightly. 'Well, perhaps not, but as a stop-gap that wouldn't matter so much.'

'I quite like the stop-gap I've got.' Olivia paused. 'But I'm sorry to have created all these difficulties. You see—I thought you'd be glad to see me.'

'Darling, I am.' He sounded eager, remorseful. 'But it's going to be bloody frustrating for both of us. So near, and yet so far apart.'

'It's not what I had in mind either,' Olivia said crisply. 'Maybe you should step your flat-hunting up a notch.'

'Yes,' he said. 'That's obviously the thing to do.' He sighed again. 'I'm going to get another drink.' He reached for her glass, and stopped. 'You've hardly touched your wine.'

'No,' she said. 'Could I have an orange juice instead, please?'

'You can have whatever you want.' He picked up her hand and kissed it. 'I'm sorry, my sweet.' His voice lowered repentantly. 'You haven't had much of a welcome, have you? But I'm still a bit stunned about all this.'

And I'm a little shaken myself, Olivia thought, watching him make his way to the bar. Because somehow, and quite unbelievably, I seem to be in league with Declan Malone.

And that has to be seriously bad news.

CHAPTER FOUR

By the time Jeremy returned with the drinks, Olivia had managed to recover her composure. She was also determined to hide her disappointment at his initial reaction to her great surprise.

Beth had clearly been right, she thought rather sadly. She should indeed have discussed her plans with him in advance. In which case she would probably still be in Bristol, a small voice in her head added brutally.

But I'm here, Olivia thought, straightening her shoulders and lifting her chin. And I'm staying.

'This temping work,' Jeremy said abruptly, setting down the glasses. 'I wish I could help, darling, but we're fully staffed at the agency. You do understand?'

'No problem.' Olivia smiled with more confidence than she actually felt, concealing her instinctive pang of hurt. 'I wasn't looking for hand-outs. I can make my own way.'

'But you're taking a hell of a risk.' He swallowed some of his drink. 'You had an established business in Bristol. You were doing really well. I can't believe you've thrown it all away like this.'

Olivia lifted her eyebrows. 'Is that how you see it? I thought I was coming to join the man I love. That was my priority.'

'Well, of course.' He reddened slightly. 'And don't think I'm not flattered.'

'I'm relieved to hear you say it.' Olivia put a hand on his knee. She said gently, 'Jeremy, I haven't come to make waves—I promise. But I felt it was time to move on—professionally as well as personally. London's still the mag-

net—the magic place. Maybe I came for myself as well—
to prove I could make it in the big city.'

'Then I hope you're not disappointed,' he said moodily.
'It isn't as easy as it seems.'

She gave him a quick, concerned glance. 'But you're all
right, aren't you? Things are going well?'

'Absolutely. Couldn't be better.' He looked at his watch.
'Apropos of which, I have to be moving. I have a business
dinner with some potential clients.'

'You do?' This time she couldn't conceal the chagrin in
her voice. 'But I thought we'd be able to spend the evening
together.'

'Not this time, my love.' He stroked her cheek swiftly,
coaxingly. 'You must realise I have appointments—commitments.'

And what about your commitment to me? she wanted to
cry out, but did not dare.

'Now, if I'd had some warning,' he went on, 'I might
have been able to rearrange my diary, perhaps.' He smiled
into her eyes. 'But we have plenty of time ahead of us—
all the time in the world, in fact.'

'So when will I see you?' Flatly, Olivia watched him
retrieve his briefcase.

'I'll call you.' He pulled her towards him, kissed her
swiftly and hotly. 'God,' he breathed, 'if there was something I could do to unload tonight's shindig—but there it
is...'

She watched him thread his way through the crowd, and
out on to the sunlit pavement.

And thought, That's that.

She could remember as a child looking forward to things—
a party, a particular birthday—with almost painful intensity,
and finding that the occasion rarely lived up to her expectations.

She had the same feeling of deflation now as she made
her way back to Notting Hill.

It was also her first experience of London's rush hour, and as she stood, strap-hanging, pressed uncomfortably between the unyielding frames of two complete strangers, she began to question her own wisdom.

Maybe she should just return quietly to Bristol and wait for Jeremy to call the shots, she thought unhappily. That was what everyone seemed to think she should do.

Including, of course, Declan Malone, she realised, wishing she had sufficient room to grind her teeth.

He was the snake in her grass—the thorn in her flesh—the something nasty in her woodshed. And she was damned if she'd give him the satisfaction of knowing that she'd trailed home with her tail between her legs. She could just imagine that cold smile of his. Well, she would do her utmost to ensure that he never smiled again.

Yes, she'd suffered a setback, but that was no reason at all to cut and run. Far better to confront her new life head-on. To take it by the scruff of the neck and shake it into line. And prove to Jeremy that she wasn't going to be some kind of drag. That she could stand beside him and play an equal part in their relationship.

And for starters she would fight her way to the door of this train, using shoulders, elbows and even teeth if she had to.

When she'd eaten her evening meal and cleared away, determinedly not dwelling on any 'might have been,' Olivia set up her laptop computer and began to compose another CV to distribute to recruitment agencies. It would do no harm to concentrate on her career prospects for a while, and let her personal life take care of itself. Maybe Jeremy needed some time to recover from the shock of her arrival, she thought drily. And he'd have more respect for her, too, if she showed her independence.

And so might Declan Malone.

She stopped, her fingers poised above the keyboard,

wondering what could have brought that unwelcome idea into her mind.

After all, it was a matter of complete indifference what that creature thought about her. But it was clear, from what Jeremy had said, that he had been giving her at least some consideration.

She sat back, frowning heavily. He'd let her off the hook with Jeremy. He'd had the chance to do her some real damage, to put in the knife and twist it, and yet he'd refrained. But why?

That was the question for which she could find no answer.

But it certainly wasn't out of the kindness of his heart, she thought sombrely. She'd seen him in action on television, after all, reducing some luckless politician to a shadow of his former self with total ruthlessness.

Admittedly she'd never been a regular viewer of the programme, because she'd no real taste for blood sports, which was probably why she hadn't recognised him at once.

On the other hand, she couldn't have expected to come face to face with a media celebrity on her first day in London, when all she'd been able to think of was Jeremy anyway.

She supposed that the reason she'd got off lightly so far was that he kept his steel for worthier foes than herself.

But that could change at any time, she acknowledged without pleasure, remembering the hard lines of his mouth, and the cold silvery glint in his eyes.

Yet his mouth could soften to warmth and charm. She'd seen it do so with other women—or at least the blonde he'd been wining and dining the other night.

She closed her eyes with a slight shiver, trying to banish that particular memory, and instead found herself wondering how his lips would feel—if they touched hers—in a kiss. How it would be to stand held intimately close against his lean body.

For a moment she could almost breathe the fresh, salty

scent of his skin, that she'd fleetingly encountered when he'd stood behind her at the window, that first morning at his house.

Until this moment she'd never realised that she had such total physical recall, making her body stir and warm with sudden, devastating need.

She leaned back in her chair, hands clasped behind her head, allowing the crisp material of her shirt to stretch tantalisingly across her hardening nipples. Imagining, as her body slackened—moistened—that it was the brush of a man's fingers—his mouth—his tongue creating this arousing torment.

But what man?

Olivia shot bolt-upright, her mouth dry, her heart pounding.

My God, she thought, am I going crazy? Only a few hours ago I was reunited with Jeremy, the man I love. The man I plan to spend the rest of my life with. Now I'm having sexual fantasies about a guy I don't even like. What's happening here?

She could not, of course, deny that Declan Malone was a seriously attractive man, with a high-flying career that only added to his charisma.

But what she was experiencing was the shameful equivalent of a schoolgirl crush, she told herself forcefully. People were being turned on all the time by complete strangers. That was how rock singers and film stars made their money. Yet that was safe—and harmless.

Contemplating what Declan Malone would be like in bed was not. That bordered on emotional infidelity to Jeremy.

And if the evening had gone according to plan it would have been Jeremy's arms around her in total reality, she reminded herself. Jeremy kissing and arousing her to the point where sanity crumbled and left only sensation.

But of course it hadn't worked out like that at all.

No point in pretending their reunion hadn't been a letdown. All her high hopes left stranded.

But she could hardly have expected Jeremy to jettison a business engagement in order to spend time with her, she told herself resolutely. Nor would she have allowed him to do so.

What niggled was that he hadn't even offered to rearrange his schedule for her sake. All she'd got was a vague promise for the future...

Olivia drew a deep breath. For heaven's sake, she wasn't giving him a chance, she reproved herself. After all, she was the one who'd chosen to pop up unexpectedly, and she had to live with the consequences.

And poor Jeremy was probably just as frustrated as she was...

And that's exactly what's wrong, she thought, her spirits rising mercurially. What you're suffering from, you idiot, is a mega-dose of sexual frustration. And because you can't have the man you want, you've simply transferred your feelings—targeted someone else.

Culpable, but no real harm done.

Because if Declan Malone was delivered to me giftwrapped, I'd send him back.

And, with a small fierce nod, she reapplied herself to her résumé with studied concentration, so much so, in fact, that when she'd finished she found herself with a slight headache.

She got up, flexing her aching shoulders. The basement felt stuffy, and slightly claustrophobic all of a sudden.

She thought, I need some fresh air.

She picked up the key for the garden, and set off up the steps.

Because it was late, she kept to the outside path, and the pools of light spilling from the uncurtained windows of the houses. Clearly no one was concerned about Peeping Toms, she realised wryly, resisting the temptation to study the brightly lit interiors as she passed, and see how the other half lived.

She wouldn't walk too far, she assured herself. Just

enough to dispel the faint muzziness from her head and
ensure she slept properly—and without any untoward
dreams.

A faint breeze stirred the air, and brought the scent of
flowers. Jasmine, she thought, breathing it longingly, her
mind torn back to her West Country home.

If she pretended really hard, maybe she could imagine
she was back there—and safe.

Now why did I think that? she wondered, her brows
snapping together sharply. I'm fine where I am. I'm content, and will be happy.

And she quickened her stride impatiently, in the process
nearly falling over a cat that had just meandered out of the
bushes in front of her, his tail held aloft like a flag.

'Whoops.' Olivia caught at an overhanging branch to
steady herself, while the cat began to wind itself round her
legs, purring furiously. She looked more closely. 'Haven't
we met before?'

From the glimpse she'd caught the day before, it looked
like the one Humph had chased—the Fosters' Maximilian.

'Hi, there.' She bent and stroked him. 'Does anyone call
you Max?'

It seemed someone did, because he chirruped at her, and
pressed even closer, arching his back in ecstasy.

'You're such a flatterer.' Olivia ran her hand along the
silky fur in a valedictory gesture. It was time she was turning back, she thought with faint unease. As it was, she'd
walked further than she'd intended. If Maximilian was
around, she was close to enemy territory.

'Stealing cats as well as husbands, Miss Butler?'

The mocking drawl made her straighten with a gasp, staring with disbelief to where he stood, a shadow on the edge
of deeper shadows.

My God, she thought, her nails scoring the palms of her
hands. I have no luck at all.

Aloud, she said coolly, 'Just making friends, Mr
Malone.'

'Where would you be without the animal kingdom?' Declan said silkily. 'I thought you'd come to worship at the shrine, perhaps.' His voice sank. ' "*But soft! what light through yonder window breaks? It is the east*"—and Jeremy is the sun. Only you're unfortunate, because he's not up in his room at the moment,' he added prosaically. 'In fact, he's out.'

'Yes,' Olivia said between her teeth. 'I know.'

'Ah,' he said. 'You've seen him, then.'

'Naturally.' She stiffened, angrily aware that she was standing in a patch of light from a neighbouring window, and that he could see her as clear as day while she couldn't see him at all. Which gave him a totally unfair advantage— as usual.

'Oh, I understand,' he said. 'You've come to thank me.'

'Thank you for what?' Olivia snapped.

'For keeping your ill-advised confidence to myself, perhaps.' His tone was dry.

'Oh,' she said, and swallowed. 'Yes.' She paused. 'Why didn't you tell him?'

'I'm not completely sure,' he said slowly. 'But it certainly wasn't out of the goodness of my heart.'

'You do surprise me.' Her voice was laced with sarcasm.

'I thought I might,' he agreed. 'And, just for the record, you also surprised Jeremy. If I wasn't the soul of charity, I'd even say you gave him a nasty shock. But perhaps that's how true love affects some people.'

'It's easy to see it's never affected you,' she flashed.

'I wouldn't argue with you there.' There was a grin in his voice the darkness couldn't hide. 'Maybe I'm not the type for grand passions. After all, they make the place look so untidy.'

'Don't you care about anything?' she demanded.

'Yes, of course. I care deeply about the integrity of my work. And I love my family,' he added, with a touch of grimness.

Olivia bit her lip. 'But all the same you've decided not

to say anything—to Jeremy?' She felt as if she were standing in a spotlight, naked, defenceless. All her emotions exposed to his merciless gaze.

'Let's say I've decided to let nature take its course,' Declan said blandly.

It wasn't a satisfactory answer, but something told her it was the best she was likely to get. Also, to get out while the going was good.

She said stiltedly, 'It's getting late. I must get back. Goodnight.'

'Going already?' He sounded disappointed. 'I thought at the very least you'd hang on and serenade the man beneath his window. Perhaps I'm the true romantic after all.'

'You, Mr Malone?' Olivia tilted her chin scornfully. 'You haven't one romantic bone in your body.'

'Nevertheless,' he said softly, 'if you'd travelled a couple of hundred miles to see me, you wouldn't be alone in bed tonight. So sleep on that, Miss Butler.'

The shadows moved, and he was gone.

For a moment Olivia was completely rigid, staring after him. Then she turned slowly and made her way back to her basement, furiously aware that her heart was pounding and her cheeks felt as if they were on fire.

'Damn him,' she muttered as she locked the gate behind her. 'Damn him to hell—and back again.'

In spite of everything, the fresh air did its work, and instead of lying awake brooding, as she'd half expected, Olivia slept almost as soon as her head touched the pillow.

She was eventually woken by her mobile phone.

Jeremy, she thought, snatching it up, but instead it was Sandra Wilton, calling to offer her a job.

'Bit of an emergency, this one,' she announced. 'One of our small business clients—he runs a property rental office in partnership with his wife, who's sprained her ankle. He needs someone to step into the breach until she can make

it back into work, so it's not a long-term proposition. I'd
say a couple of days at most.

'It's also quite close to you—Kensington High Street.
Can I tell him you're on your way?'

'What would I be expected to do?' Olivia asked, noting
down the name and address.

Sandra chuckled. 'Apparently it's Mrs Sutton who knows
how the computer works, so poor Colin is currently climbing the wall. You'll earn your money if you can show him
how to get into his database and perform a few simple
functions.'

Sandra had not exaggerated. On her arrival at Personal
Property, Olivia found a tall, elegantly dressed man with
greying hair eying the computer as if it were a poisonous
snake.

'Vicky told me what to do,' he said wretchedly, once
they'd introduced themselves, 'what keys to press and all
that, but it doesn't seem to respond. I think I've broken it.'

Olivia smiled at him soothingly. 'Let me see what I can
do,' she said, unobtrusively switching on the power source.

'My God.' Colin Sutton stared at the sudden burst of
activity on the screen. 'How did you manage that?'

Olivia kept her face straight. 'Just a lucky guess,' she
said gently. 'Now, where do you want me to start?'

As the name of their business suggested, the Suttons offered a property search service, matching people carefully
with their accommodation requirements, and managing the
rental arrangements thereafter.

'Our clients like to feel they're being treated as individ-
uals, whether they're landlords or tenants,' Colin Sutton
explained. 'A lot of our properties are owned by people
working abroad, and they have the reassurance of knowing
their homes are going to be occupied by tenants who appreciate them, and respect them too. Our aim is to keep the
whole thing as trouble-free as possible.'

Personal Property was clearly a thriving business. The
phone rang constantly, and there was a steady stream of

callers too. During the afternoon, when it was quieter, Mr Sutton went to look at two flats the company was being asked to manage, and Olivia held the fort alone.

It gave her the chance to browse through the register of available properties and print off the details of three or four which she hoped might interest Jeremy. That was if they were in the right area, she amended ruefully.

Her brows rose when she saw the rents, but by the time they moved in she would have regular work and be able to make a proper contribution, she told herself.

But the real shock came when she found a basement bedsit, almost identical to her own, and in the Lancey Gardens neighbourhood, costing twice what she was paying.

When Colin Sutton returned, she asked rather shyly if it was a mistake.

'Far from it,' he told her briskly. 'That's one of the cheaper ones.'

Which gave Olivia serious food for thought as she went home that evening, having assured an anxious Mr Sutton that she would be back sharp at nine the following morning.

On the way down to her basement, she knocked at Sasha's door, intending to have it out with her, but there was no reply.

She's probably taking Humph for a walk, thought Olivia. I'll write her a note and pop it through the door.

She composed her letter carefully, saying merely that she wished to discuss the rent, and would be grateful if Sasha could spare her some time that evening.

She'd shopped during her lunch-break, and now set about preparing her evening meal—pork steak casseroled with tomatoes, onions, mushrooms and wine.

When it was all simmering nicely, she decided to have a shower. She'd just finished, and, wrapped in her bathrobe, was towelling her hair vigorously, when there was a knock at the door.

Sasha, she thought, tossing the damp towel on to a chair.

But as she opened the door her welcoming smile died on her lips and she took a step backwards, gazing with stupefaction at Declan Malone.

'You?' she said. 'What are you doing here?'

'I came to see you about this.'

Olivia saw with outrage that he was holding up her note.

'Do you usually read other people's private correspondence?' she demanded icily.

'Only when I'm asked,' he said with equal coldness. 'Sasha hates wearing glasses, and avoids doing so at all costs, although she can't read a word without them. So I told her it was a double glazing hand-out.'

Olivia gasped. 'Well, how dare you?'

'And how dare you?' he came back at her sharply. 'She's charging you little enough as it is, but you want to beat her down still further, you mercenary little cat. And because she's got a heart like putty she'd probably let you get away with it.'

For a moment Olivia was stunned, but only for a moment. Then anger took over.

'Oh, you have me completely summed up,' she said, her tone heavy with irony. 'There's nothing I enjoy more than defrauding people who've been kind to me. That's when I'm not stealing from orphans and mugging pensioners, of course.' Her voice nearly cracked. 'Now get out of here.'

'I'm going nowhere.' He walked in, and closed the door behind him. 'Look, maybe I was a bit harsh...'

'Maybe?' Olivia choked out a savage laugh. 'Oh, not you. You're devoted to the integrity of your work—remember? Being judge, jury and executioner all rolled into one, and most impressive—as long as you're not on the receiving end.'

She swallowed. 'And I suppose it becomes such a habit it spills over into your private life too,' she added furiously.

'Not,' he said slowly, 'that anyone's ever told me.'

'They wouldn't dare.' The tendrils of her hair felt damp

against her neck, and she was acutely conscious that the robe was her only covering.

Declan's mouth tightened. 'I can appreciate you may be having financial difficulties,' he said, after a pause. 'London prices are always a shock to anyone moving up from the provinces. However...'

'However—nothing.' Olivia lifted her chin. 'And kindly don't patronise me. I didn't come here on a wing and a prayer. And I'm not some indigent, looking for charity either,' she added heatedly. 'I'm perfectly able to pay the rent Sasha's asked for. But I'm temping at a rental agency, and my concern is that she's not charging enough. That she doesn't realise how much the market average has risen. That's what I wanted to talk to her about.'

She paused, glaring at him. 'Not that it's any concern of yours.'

'You forget, I sent you to her. That makes me responsible.'

'Oh, let's hear it for the Good Samaritan.' She was trembling. 'Now, please leave.'

'Not until we've sorted this out.' He picked up the towel and held it out to her. 'You're getting cold. Go and dress, then we'll talk.'

'And why should I?'

'Because I don't want you catching pneumonia and laying it at my door,' Declan retorted. 'Off with you, now.'

She gave him a mutinous look, then headed for the bathroom, grabbing jeans and a sweatshirt as she went.

She dragged on her clothes, then brushed her hair back from her face with severity, confining it at the nape of her neck with an elastic band.

For once he'd be confronted by a woman who wouldn't dress—or undress—to please him, she thought, giving her reflection a curt nod of approval.

Declan was lounging in the armchair, but as Olivia came back into the room he rose to his feet.

'I turned down the light under the pan on the stove,' he said. 'I didn't want your dinner to burn.'

'Checking that I can afford food?'

Declan lifted his hands in a resigned gesture. 'Let's call a truce, for God's sake. All right—I misjudged your motives over the rent; I admit it.'

'But in light of all my other vices you thought you were justified.' Her voice was bitter. 'How was it you saw my letter anyway? What were you doing round at Sasha's? Spying on me, I suppose?'

'Don't over-estimate your importance,' Declan told her curtly. 'I help Sasha every month with her household accounts. Book-keeping isn't her strong suit.'

'I'm not surprised—when she doesn't even charge economic rents.'

'She may not have the soul of an accountant,' Declan said, after a pause, 'but she possesses a kind heart in abundance. She charges what she thinks people can manage to pay. She likes to have the rooms occupied. Making a profit isn't her prime concern.'

'But how can she afford to do that?' Olivia objected. 'She must have outgoings—building maintenance. Does she work?'

'She doesn't act on the stage any more,' he said. 'But she's still in demand for radio, and voice-overs.'

'Oh, I see.' Olivia wasn't sure that she did. 'And does she earn enough from that?'

'Probably not. But she has a private income in addition.' Declan raised his brows. 'Is there anything else you'd like to know?'

Olivia flushed. 'You think I'm prying, but I just want to make sure she's not missing out by keeping me here.'

'You don't need to worry,' he said laconically. 'And, after all, it won't be for long—will it?' The cool eyes flashed silver at her.

Olivia's throat felt suddenly constricted. 'No—I hope

not,' she muttered, hating his derisive smile. She frowned slightly. 'But I still don't understand your involvement.'

'You don't have to. Let's just say I'm an old friend.'

'She's very lucky.' The words were spoken before she knew it. The colour in her face deepened uncontrollably. 'I mean, you lead such a busy life. It's surprising you have the time.'

'I can always make time for people I love.' He spoke quietly.

Their eyes met, and held. Olivia felt her breathing shorten as her whole body tensed in sudden, inexplicable excitement.

Such a brief distance between them in physical terms, she thought, swallowing. Yet in reality they stood on either side of an uncrossable abyss.

She wondered crazily what would happen if she took a step towards him—and another...

Her lips parted to speak, although she had no idea what she was going to say. Then the heated silence was pierced—destroyed by the shrilling of her mobile phone.

'Oh.' She dived for it. Pressed the answer button.

'Darling.' It was Jeremy's voice. 'I've just realised I'm free tonight. Why don't we have dinner?'

She could think of a whole number of reasons, not the least being her casserole, which was filling the flat with its beguiling aroma. And not being taken so completely for granted featured prominently too.

She paused her eyes going again to Declan, who had risen from his seat. He looked back at her, brows lifting, mouth twisting scornfully.

It was that look which did it. Which decided her to ignore the fact that she was obviously an afterthought and take Jeremy up on his invitation after all.

To hell with Declan Malone. Let him think what he wanted.

'That would be wonderful.' Deliberately, she let her

voice caress the words, her answering glance defiant. 'I can hardly wait.'

She heard Declan make a small, angry sound in his throat, then he turned sharply and went to the door, slamming it behind him.

'What was that?' Jeremy demanded.

'Nothing,' Olivia said, crossing her fingers. 'Nothing at all. Oh, darling, I'm so glad to hear from you.'

And that, she thought, was at least the truth.

But she didn't want to examine too closely why she felt that Jeremy's call could have been a lifeline, thrown at exactly the right moment.

Because she didn't need saving, she told herself resolutely. She was fine, and well in control of the situation—wasn't she?

CHAPTER FIVE

JEREMY took her to a restaurant on the King's Road—much patronised by young trendies, he informed her, with a trace of patronage himself.

Olivia, who'd rapidly changed into a shift dress the colour of wheat, topping it with a dark brown and white striped jacket, felt seriously overdressed amongst the grungy colours favoured by the rest of the clientele.

Again, it wasn't the most romantic rendezvous he could have chosen either, she thought rather sadly. It was brightly lit, noisy and overcrowded, and the food was ordinary in the extreme.

But then, as he said, it was the kind of place where you came to be seen, she rationalised, as she dutifully ate her burger and the rather stingy portion of fries which accompanied it.

While they drank their coffee, Olivia handed over the details of the flats she'd picked up that day, and Jeremy received them with raised eyebrows.

'You don't waste much time,' he commented in a slightly aggrieved tone. 'I was going to start looking next week.'

'It just seemed such a splendid opportunity.' Olivia heard and despised the placatory note in her voice.

'Hmm.' He scanned the sheets rapidly. 'Actually, I've heard of these people. They've a good reputation. I'll bear them in mind.' He folded the papers and put them into an inside pocket of his jacket. 'But don't you think you should find a permanent job before we go any further? I mean, temping isn't the most stable of livings.'

'I've already thought of that.' Olivia smiled at him. 'I

don't see why I shouldn't continue what I was doing in Bristol—training people in computer systems.'

Jeremy gave her a pitying look. 'I doubt you'd find much call for that in London. People are pretty clued up here, not like the provinces.'

That's what you think, thought Olivia, remembering Colin Sutton's anguished expression.

'Although you might find something in office administration, when you've a little more experience,' he added kindly. 'Don't try to run before you can walk, Livvy.'

Thanks for the encouragement, Olivia thought forlornly.

She said, 'You're probably right.' Then, to the hovering waitress, 'No more coffee, thanks.'

Olivia had hoped they'd walk along the King's Road for a while, talk, recapture some of the old magic, but Jeremy immediately hailed a taxi.

'You can show me this flat of yours,' he whispered ardently, his lips brushing her ear as the cab drew away.

'You said it wouldn't be safe,' Olivia reminded him, very conscious of the driver's presence.

'To hell with that.' His voice thickened. 'I'm not waiting any longer. Oh, God, Livvy...' He took her into his arms, kissing her passionately, while one hand stole beneath her jacket to stroke her breasts.

She was passive in his arms, neither resisting his advances nor particularly welcoming them either, wishing with all her heart that he'd waited until they were alone. Especially when his fingers slid under the edge of her skirt.

'Jeremy.' She pushed away the exploring hand. 'He'll see.'

'Don't be such a prude,' he teased. 'Cab drivers see this every day.'

'Not from me they don't,' Olivia told him with hauteur.

'Have it your own way,' he said with a touch of impatience. 'But you'd better loosen up a little when we get back.'

She flinched inwardly. This was going to be their first

time together. She wanted it to mean as much to him as it did to her. Not just some graceless coupling as thanks for an indifferent meal.

Slowly, she unlocked her door, while Jeremy paid off the cab.

'Well, this is it.' There was a nervous tremor in her voice as he followed her in. She moved towards the kitchen, trying not to hurry. 'Would you like some more coffee?'

'There's only one thing I want,' he said softly, his smiling glance traversing her body, stripping her naked. 'Don't play hard to get, Livvy. Not now we're finally together.'

'We've been apart for several months,' she reminded him, her throat tightening. 'Maybe we should get to know each other again first.'

'The best way to renew acquaintance is in bed,' he told her throatily. He pulled her towards him, slipping her jacket off her shoulders and tugging down the zip of her dress almost with the same practised movement. 'I want to look at you, darling, every sweet, desirable inch of you,' he muttered huskily.

She backed away, holding on to her dress, trying to laugh. 'Now wait a minute…'

'That's all I've ever done—from the moment we met.' He sounded petulant, even angry. 'But enough's enough. Tonight you're going to come through, Livvy.'

She'd reached the wall. Her back was against it. There was nowhere else to retreat to. And Jeremy had reached her, fumbling with his clothing.

'As there doesn't seem to be a bed,' he said, grinning wolfishly. 'This will have to do, my love.'

'No.' Olivia twisted under his grasp. He was, she realised, totally aroused—and determined. Whereas she…

My God, she thought. Surely I'm worth more than this—a quickie up against a wall.

The sudden knocking at the door was like the answer to a prayer.

She found herself thinking, Declan?

Then heard Sasha's voice. 'Olivia, are you all right? Humph has been barking—as if there's a prowler. May I come in?'

'Just a minute.' Olivia ducked under Jeremy's arm, feverishly rezipping her dress.

'It's my landlady. You'd better go in the bathroom,' she whispered to him.

'Get rid of her,' he mouthed savagely back at her as he obeyed.

Olivia went to the door, combing her fingers through her hair.

'Dear girl,' Sasha said as she came in. 'Humph is making such a fuss, I thought I'd better check on you. Have you seen or heard anything peculiar? Have any strangers been hanging around?'

She was looking her usual exotic self, in slim-fitting black trousers and a tunic top embroidered with poppies, with a black bandanna tied round her hair. She glanced around as she spoke, the bright eyes missing nothing.

'Everything's fine,' said Olivia, torn between conflicting emotions of annoyance and amusement, commingled with relief. She didn't believe there was a possible prowler for one moment. Sasha, she had no doubt, was acting on Declan's instructions. 'Humph just heard me come home, I expect.'

'Oh, he's used to you,' Sasha said dismissively. 'He only sounds off if he hears a footstep—or a voice—he doesn't recognise.'

She gave Olivia a searching look. 'You seem rather flushed, darling. Are you running a temperature? Of course, it has been warm for the time of year.'

'That must be it,' Olivia agreed gravely.

'It's so nerve-racking living on your own,' Sasha went on, with a sigh. 'Declan says I should install panic buttons down here, and in my own part of the house, in case of problems, and I'm sure he's right.' She gave Olivia one of her blinding smiles. 'But you've got your little mobile phone, haven't you, darling? So if you get nervous at any time you can always call me.'

'I'll bear that in mind,' Olivia promised as Sasha flitted to the door and, with one last smile over her shoulder, vanished.

'What was that all about?' Jeremy demanded sourly, emerging from the bathroom.

Olivia sighed. 'I think she was telling me she knew you were here.'

Jeremy muttered an obscenity. 'I knew she'd be spying for bloody Declan,' he said vengefully. He gave his surroundings a cursory look. 'Well, this is clearly a non-starter as a love-nest. I'll have to think of something else. See if I can borrow a key from someone who's going on holiday.'

Olivia bit her lip. 'I don't think I'd be very happy with that.'

'What's the matter with you?' He stared at her. 'You come all this way to be with me, and now you're backing off.'

'I came all this way so that we could live together, openly and permanently.' Olivia lifted her chin. 'Not to have a squalid secret affair in other people's beds.'

There was a taut silence, then Jeremy pursed his lips in resignation.

'You're quite right, of course,' he said repentantly. 'I'm sorry, darling, I've been thinking and acting like a sex-starved lout. It's just that I want you so much, yet I still have to go on waiting. It's like a life sentence.'

He held out his arms, and Olivia went into them.

'It's frustrating for me too,' she reminded him softly. 'But we do have the rest of our lives to get it right.'

'Yes, I know.' His kiss was gentle this time, but brief. 'Now I'd better go, before Mata Hari pays us another visit.' He gave a boyish laugh. 'We'll just have to content ourselves with an old-fashioned courtship—walks in the park, trips to the zoo—the whole bit.'

'Sounds good to me,' she assured him tenderly.

He lifted her hand to his lips. 'I'll call you,' he said, and left.

Olivia stood for a moment, looking at the closed door and listening to the silence.

It had not been the easiest evening of her life, she acknowledged ruefully. For a while she'd been shocked— even repelled—by Jeremy's behaviour. He seemed to have turned into a coarse, unpleasant stranger.

But the present circumstances were difficult for them both, she thought, as she began the nightly ritual of locking up. And maybe this bad beginning would have a good ending if it prompted Jeremy to find a flat of his own. That would be the answer to everything.

Declan could interfere as much as he chose, she told herself defiantly, but everything was going to be all right. She knew it.

Wednesday began with another busy morning at Personal Property. However, Olivia came back from her lunch-break to the news that Vicky Sutton could manage to hobble on her damaged ankle, and would be returning the following day.

'She thinks the place falls apart without her,' Colin confided with obvious affection. 'And she could be right.' He paused. 'I've told your agency, and they have another job for you to go to. Call them when you have a moment.'

Olivia, whose heart had begun to sink, revived at these words.

Sandra Wilton didn't beat about the bush when she contacted her.

'I'm sending you to Academy Productions tomorrow,' she said. 'We already have one of our older temps working there, someone who retrained after having a family, and I think she's struggling a bit.'

She paused. 'They've asked for a PA, because theirs is off sick, but I suspect you'll be answering phones, doing reception, making coffee, and fetching the sandwiches.'

'Oh,' said Olivia, and Sandra chuckled.

'Not your scene, I know, but the money's good, and they use us regularly, so something better might come your way if you hang in there.' She hesitated. 'And I'd be glad if you'd keep an eye on Barbara—give her back-up if she needs it. I think her confidence has taken a bit of a battering over the past couple of days.'

'What kind of company is it?'

'An independent outfit, making drama and documentaries for the major television networks. They've won awards, so they're good, and most of the girls like going there. It's casual dress and plenty of buzz.'

Academy Productions was housed in a small square just off Marylebone, occupying the first and second floor of a block which had been formed originally by knocking several old houses together.

The ground floor itself was occupied by an antiques shop, a florist's, and a second-hand bookshop, and there was a glass door at the side protected by a buzzer system with the name of the production company blazoned upon it.

Olivia duly announced herself, and went up a narrow flight of stairs to yet another door, where a small dark-haired girl was waiting.

'Hi,' she said unsmilingly. 'I'm Carol from Admin and I'm here to show you round and get you started.' She paused. 'I hope you do better than your colleague.'

Not a promising start, Olivia reflected, as she obediently hung her jacket on one of the pegs in the women's rest-room.

It was a large open-plan office, well-lit and comfortable with plenty of greenery around, but, rather than the 'buzz' Sandra had referred to, there was an atmosphere of tension you could cut with a knife, Olivia thought as she followed Carol to the front desk, where she'd be starting the day.

'Do you know how this kind of switchboard works?' Carol asked, and appeared marginally reassured by Olivia's nod. 'All the extension numbers are listed here, and if you get into difficulties, scream for help. Don't pretend you can cope. Mimi, one of our part-timers, will be in later to give you a hand.'

She paused. 'We get a lot of calls from wannabes, so anyone who can't give you a contact name is always shunted to Extension 39 for sorting. And absolutely everyone who asks for J.L. must be routed through Paula, his secretary. She knows who he'll want to talk to.'

Olivia made a quick note on the pad in front of her. 'Right.'

'The main door is deliveries, which you check on this screen, and appointments only. You'll find them all listed on the computer.

'And don't worry too much about getting outside numbers for people,' Carol went on. 'Most of them will ask for a line and make their own calls.' She frowned. 'Having said that, will you get on to Hogarth Systems—you'll find their number in the Rolodex—and ask them to send a technician? I've been calling since I got in and their number seems permanently engaged.'

She added a wintry smile, and disappeared.

Well, at least she didn't mention making coffee, Olivia thought, as the telephone began to ring. But if they were all like her, it was no wonder the place seemed fraught.

She felt absurdly nervous, as if everyone was expecting her to fail, but there were no glitches. Whenever she was free, she dialled the number that Carol had requested, but when she eventually got through she found she was connected to an answering machine. She left the company name and number and asked them to make contact urgently.

Mimi arrived at ten-thirty, a tall slim girl with skin like ebony. She wore her hair in dozens of tiny beaded braids, and her skirt skimmed her thighs.

'I'll cover for you,' she said. 'Did Caring Carol show you where to take a break? No? What a bloody surprise.' She pointed. 'Go to the end of that aisle, and there's a door on the left. That's the kitchen. There's coffee, tea, soft drinks in the fridge. Help yourself, and can you bring me a coffee back—white no sugar?'

'Thanks.' Olivia hesitated. 'There's another girl from the agency here. Do you know where she works so I can say hello? Her name's Barbara.'

Mimi pulled a face. 'You might find her in the kitchen, weeping into a hot chocolate, or in the restroom using up a week's supply of tissues. She's not flavour of the month just now.'

'What did she do?'

Mimi rolled expressive eyes to heaven. 'Oh, not much. Just lost two draft scripts and the notes for an entire series last night. She was supposed to be using Scriptec, and she's only learned Word for Windows—result, disaster. Now someone's had to explain to one of our star performers that several weeks' work has gone down the tubes and he has to start all over again.' She shook her head. 'I don't think he'll be pleased.'

'My God,' said Olivia.

Barbara was indeed in the kitchen, a pleasant-faced woman in her early forties, clutching a mug of cold tea as if it was her sole hold on reality.

Olivia checked in the doorway. 'Hi,' she said. 'I work for Service Group too. Is there anything I can do to help?'

The other shook her head. 'It's too late for that. I feel terrible. This is my first job, and I did so want it to go well.' There was a little sob in her voice.

Olivia came to sit opposite her at the table. 'Perhaps it isn't as bad as you think.'

'Not as bad?' Barbara stared at her tragically. 'Do you know what I did? I was given this disk, and told to download it on to another master disk. They asked if I knew how, and I said yes, because it never occurred to me that Scriptec was that different. I thought I'd be able to work it out. But I couldn't, and I started to panic, and I ended up wiping both of them.'

A tear trickled down her face. 'And now they'll tell the agency, and Sandra will probably sack me, and I'll have to go home and tell them all that I've failed.'

'Don't get upset,' Olivia said gently.

'I can't help it. You see, I was really thrilled to be working on this project, because the man fronting it is one of my favourites. He's a real professional. I watch all his programmes, but Derek, my husband, has never been keen. He's always said that he reckoned he could be really nasty—and that he wouldn't like to cross him. And now I have,' she added on a little wail.

'Not necessarily,' Olivia said patiently. 'Do you know how genuinely hard it is to lose things permanently inside a computer?

'And besides,' she went on, warming to her theme, 'it's partly his own fault. If he was a real professional he'd keep back-up disks, and if he hasn't he's an incompetent idiot.'

She gave Barbara an encouraging smile, but the older woman wasn't even looking at her. She was staring past Olivia towards the doorway, with an expression that suggested another *Nightmare on Elm Street* was being enacted in front of her.

Olivia suddenly felt very cold. She turned slowly in her chair, and found herself looking straight into the blazing eyes of Declan Malone.

For a moment she stared at him, unable to believe her own eyes or speak. Praying that she was suffering some kind of brainstorm—and that this wasn't really happening.

Oh, God, she thought wretchedly. Out of all the jobs in London, what vicious trick of fate had brought her here— to his production company?

'Don't stop there, Miss Butler.' His tone made ice appear human. 'I'm sure you have other valuable insights into working practice to share with us.' He paused. 'Come on, now. Don't tell me you're lost for words.'

Behind him, Olivia could see Carol, looking horrified,

and a number of other people totally agog. She wanted to run, but pride insisted she stand her ground. Brazen it out.

'Not at all, Mr Malone.' Her voice was equally frigid. 'I was just recalling what they always say about eavesdroppers. And I stick to what I said earlier. Even a beginner knows you must use back-up on computers.'

His mouth tightened angrily. 'It was an oversight. Up to now my faith in the secretarial service here has always been justified.'

Olivia cast a swift look at Barbara, who had her head buried in her hands, then got to her feet, facing Declan, her hands balling into fists at her sides.

'Start taking responsibility for your own mistakes,' she said tersely. 'And keep your bullying tactics for the television screen. It's less impressive in private.'

She reached across and touched Barbara's sleeve. 'Come on,' she said quietly. 'Let's forget the recriminations, and see what we can salvage instead.'

Carol pushed her way forward. 'I instructed this young woman to send for a technician, Declan. It seems that she's as incompetent as her colleague. But neither of them will work here again, and if Sandra Wilton wants our business in future then she'll have to fire them.'

'I left a message on the machine at Hogarth's,' Olivia returned steadily. 'But they haven't come back to us yet.' She hesitated. 'But I'm quite prepared to see what I can do.'

Carol said grimly, 'I think you've done enough already. And Mrs Wilton will get a full report, I promise you.' She turned to the grimly silent man beside her. 'Declan, I can't tell you how sorry I am about all this. And this girl's attitude simply adds insult to injury.'

'Oh, I'm accustomed to that,' he said softly. 'Miss Butler and I are old antagonists.' He looked at Olivia, and the white-faced Barbara standing beside her. 'What do you know about computers?'

'Enough,' she said. 'Your data's locked into it some-where. All I have to do is find the key.'

'Nonsense,' said Carol. 'Trust me, Declan. I'll convince Hogarth's to send a technician as a matter of urgency.'

'But if they're not answering their phone, that could take hours. And Miss Butler is here now.'

'You're surely not going to turn her loose on the com-puter?'

'Why not?' He shrugged. 'She can't actually make things any worse.' He looked at Olivia, his eyes glittering like burnished silver. 'You're on, Miss Butler. We'll go to my office.'

Olivia followed him up the stairs to the second floor, nerves tying knots in her stomach. She was dismally aware that she might have bitten off more than she could chew as Declan led her along a narrow corridor, lined on both sides with rooms hardly bigger than cubicles.

His was a corner office, and slightly larger, with a win-dow offering a view over the yard at the back, a desk lit-tered with papers, and another desk holding a state-of-the-art computer.

'It's all yours, Miss Butler.' Declan held the chair for her to sit down with elaborate courtesy. His smile was tight, and faintly scornful. He was waiting, she realised, seething, for her to fall flat on her face.

'Thank you,' she returned with equal politeness, keeping her own expression impassive. She leaned forward, switch-ing on the power, allowing the machine to boot up. 'I can't promise this will be quick.'

'Take whatever time is necessary, of course.' He paused. 'Is there anything you need?'

'You can leave that to me, Declan.' Carol had followed them. 'I intend to remain and supervise Miss Butler while she's still in the building.'

'No,' Olivia said, swiftly and decisively. 'I have to con-centrate, and I can't do that with someone breathing down my neck. I must be on my own.'

'Now just a moment—' Carol began pugnaciously, but Declan halted her with a raised hand.

'She's the expert,' he murmured, his mouth twisting. 'I suggest we go, and leave her to get on with it.'

'Just one thing,' Olivia said as he turned to go. 'The name of the missing files?'

'They're all listed under "ExPrime."' His faintly bored tone indicated that this information would probably not be required, which needled her still further.

We'll see about that, she told him silently as the door closed on him and the mutinous Carol.

But it wouldn't be easy. Scriptec wasn't a program she'd encountered much in the past, although she could see its attraction for media people. But it was undeniably tricky, and poor Barbara had been thrown in at the deep end.

But she should have asked for help, Olivia thought. Just as Declan should have copied his files. And now she had to sort out the resultant mess. Which she would do. She was completely determined about that in the face of Declan's overt scepticism. She had something important to prove.

With a sigh, she clicked on to the Scriptec program, and began methodically to search.

A computer's memory was rather like one of those Russian dolls, she thought a couple of hours later. No matter how many layers you removed, there were always more, just waiting to be discovered. And this machine had a big memory.

She was conscious of someone—it could have been Declan—bringing her a beaker of black coffee at some point, and later this was replaced by a tuna salad sandwich, and a carton of fresh orange juice.

She ate and drank on autopilot, her eyes ceaselessly scanning the screen, hunting for the block of data that was buried somewhere.

Her head was aching and her shoulders screaming with tension when she hit pay-dirt at last. Hardly daring to breathe, she brought the files on to the screen—checked them through to make sure they were complete, then carefully and meticulously saved each one in turn.

Only then, as she leaned back in her chair, did she allow her tired mouth to relax into a triumphant grin.

The door behind her opened, and Carol said sharply, 'The technician from Hogarth's is here, and he'll be taking over. So you can go.'

'My pleasure.' Olivia got up, stretching. 'But I've retrieved the scripts and they're now on disk, so make sure he doesn't lose them again.'

'You found them? I don't believe it.'

Olivia shrugged. 'That's your problem. Thankfully, I've solved mine.'

As she walked past Carol to the door she found her way blocked by Declan.

He said incredulously, 'You've got the scripts back? Show me.'

'You know which keys to press, Mr Malone.' Olivia lifted her chin. 'I'm out of here.'

She heard him say her name, but she took no notice, marching along the passage and down the stairs, pausing only to collect her jacket on the way out.

Mimi called to her. 'Olivia—they want you back on the second floor.'

'Tough,' Olivia returned succinctly, and kept going.

There was a bus stop just round the corner, and a bus coming along the road as she reached it. Olivia boarded it, not even looking to see where it was headed, and asked for the terminus.

Traffic was heavy, and it was a slow, grinding journey, giving her time to unwind a little.

Well, she'd burnt her boats at Academy Productions, she thought, and probably with the agency too, which was worse. But she'd talk to Sandra and speak up for Barbara if she got the chance. Because having to work under someone like Carol was enough to zap anyone's confidence and efficiency, she told herself. The woman was a bully.

But then she was in good company, Olivia muttered silently, with Declan Malone stalking around like Attila the Hun. And if I'd had the least idea he worked for Academy Productions I wouldn't have gone near the place. No amount of money is worth the aggravation.

Although there was every chance she wouldn't be paid a penny for today's efforts, of course, she realised, pulling a face.

In the meantime, she needed some fresh air to clear her head—or what passed for fresh air in London.

She left the bus near Regents Park, and wandered round for an hour or so, enjoying Queen Mary's Gardens and taking a look at the Open Air Theatre. Maybe she could persuade Jeremy to bring her to a production here. It occurred to her that she had no real idea whether he liked the theatre at all, let alone whether he preferred classical drama to modern plays or musicals to opera.

But that's all part of our learning process about each other, she reminded herself as she turned back to begin her tortuous journey home.

She was just leaving the park when her mobile phone rang.

'Where on earth are you?' was Sandra's greeting. 'And how does it feel to be the heroine of the hour?'

Olivia halted. 'What do you mean?'

'Apparently you dashed off before they could hand out your medal.' Sandra laughed. 'But it seems one of the girls is about to go off on maternity leave and they want you to fill in for her, so they must be impressed.'

'You're joking.' The words burst from her.

'No, I'm perfectly serious, and so are they. I heard about how you rode to the rescue, and I'm full of admiration too. So what shall I tell them?'

Olivia bit her lip. 'Can I think about it and let you know?'

'Well—yes,' Sandra said slowly. She sounded astonished. 'But what's the problem? I mean, this could be a really good contract for you—and it's a nice environment to work in.'

'Is it?' Olivia asked drily, thinking of Carol. 'Have you asked Barbara about that?'

Sandra sighed. 'Sending her there was my mistake. I'm finding her a more conventional slot, where she'll be able to relax and enjoy using her skills. But you're a different proposition. I—I really thought you'd jump at the challenge.'

'Perhaps I'd prefer a more conventional slot too,' Olivia said. She hesitated. 'Will I be black-listed if I say no?'

'Of course not. There's plenty of work about.' Sandra sounded deflated. 'But nothing as interesting.'

'Perhaps it all depends on your interests.' Olivia paused. 'But I'll be in touch as soon as I've decided.'

She switched off the phone and put it back in her bag, her mind whirling. This was the last thing she'd expected. It would almost be worth taking them up on the offer simply to see Carol's face. Except that she'd find herself looking at Declan Malone at the same time.

And that, she knew, was not a good idea, for all kinds of reasons that she didn't want to examine too closely.

If I never see him again it will be too soon, she told herself firmly.

And wondered why she had to keep convincing herself of something so self-evident.

CHAPTER SIX

SHE was still deep in thought when she turned into Lancey Terrace, and had nearly reached the house when she realised that a familiar figure was lounging against the railings.

She stopped dead, her brows snapping together in a swift frown.

'So there you are at last.' Declan came towards her.

'And here you are for no reason at all,' she countered.

'I have an excellent reason,' he said. 'Believe it or not, I've come to thank you.'

'Consider it said,' Olivia told him curtly. 'Now, if you'll excuse me, I'm going to have a shower and something to eat.'

'And also to ask you to have dinner with me.' He was blocking her way. 'And don't tell me you have a prior engagement, because it's clear you haven't.'

'No,' she said. 'But a subsequent one is always a possibility.'

'I think Jeremy is tied up with some work thing tonight.' He paused, then smiled at her. For the first time it seemed to her that he was seeing her as a real person, and—more disturbingly—a woman. She was aware of an odd frisson—something between pleasure and apprehension. An internal voice seemed to be telling her to step back—to distance herself. And yet she found that she was standing her ground.

He said gently, 'Olivia—I'm really grateful for what you did today, and I'd like to express it in some tangible way. Have dinner with me, please?'

She was silent for a moment, then she threw back her head, staring him straight in the eye. 'I'll tell you how you could thank me.' Her voice shook slightly. 'You could get off my case.'

'Pardon?' His brows lifted.

'You heard me. If you're so grateful—do that for me. Give Jeremy and me some space to make a life together. You don't have to approve—just stand back.'

He was very still, his narrowed eyes fixed on her pale face. Then he nodded, giving her a swift, crooked grin.

'It's a deal.'

'You mean it?' She was astounded.

'Yes,' he said. And shrugged. *'Qué será, será,'* he added softly. 'And now a truce has been declared, will you agree to have dinner with me—at the third time of asking?'

Instinct—reason—warned her to refuse. Words of polite denial were already forming in her mind.

Instead, she heard herself say primly, 'Thank you. I— I'd like that.'

'A slight exaggeration.' His grin widened. 'But—who knows? Maybe you'll come to mean it—one of these days.' He paused. 'Shall we say eight o'clock? I'll pick you up here.' His smile touched her startled eyes and parted lips. 'Until then,' he said, and walked away, leaving her staring after him.

As Declan let himself into his house Jeremy came out of the kitchen carrying a can of beer.

'Hi. Do you want one?'

Declan shook his head. 'I'm going out to dinner later.' He paused. 'I thought you were working tonight.'

Jeremy shrugged. 'I was supposed to be meeting a client, but it was cancelled, so I'm playing squash with Tom Bainbridge instead. I just came home to change.' He gave Declan a leering glance. 'So, who's the lucky lady tonight? One of your groupies?'

'On the contrary.' Declan felt a curl of distaste inside him. God, he thought, love must be a weird thing if it kept a sane girl like Maria wanting this oaf. And Olivia too.

'You mean she didn't fall on her back the moment you looked at her?' Jeremy gave a loud laugh. 'She must be unique.'

'Possibly.' Declan gave him a thin-lipped smile. 'Certainly deserving of my closest attention.'

'I get you.' Jeremy winked. 'No worries, old boy. I'll be the invisible man when I come back tonight.'

'Thanks,' Declan said drily. 'But that might be a little premature.'

'Playing hard to get, is she?' Jeremy's face darkened slightly. 'They're the worst.'

Ah, thought Declan, suddenly alert. So things aren't going to plan in the romance of the century. How interesting. Yet he was with her the other night. Sasha is sure of it.

Aloud, he said lightly, 'I'm taking things gently. She's—currently involved.'

'And you're going to create a diversion?' Jeremy laughed again. 'My God, you can be a bastard sometimes. She won't know what's happening to her.'

Declan gave him a tranquil smile. 'I'm counting on it,' he said. 'Now I'm going up to shower.'

'Before you go—' Jeremy cleared his throat awkwardly. 'I want you to know that I'm seriously looking for a place of my own.'

Declan halted, one foot on the bottom stair. 'Any particular reason?' he asked, brows raised.

Jeremy did not meet his eyes. 'It's been good of you to have me here—but it's time I went. You want your privacy, and I—I need my independence.'

Declan nodded expressionlessly. 'What does Maria think?'

Jeremy looked more uncomfortable than ever. 'Well, I haven't really discussed it with her. I thought I'd see a few flats—narrow the choice a little first.' He gave an unconvincing laugh. 'After all—you know women.'

'I've known some,' Declan agreed, thoughtfully. 'Well—good luck with the hunt.'

'And good luck with yours too, old boy.' Jeremy lifted his beer can in a parody of a toast, then went back into the kitchen.

Declan went up to his room, thinking furiously. He'd lay odds that Jeremy wasn't planning to set up house with his wife, he told himself grimly. So his decision to make a play for Olivia, to use himself as bait to lure her from Jeremy, hadn't been made a moment too soon.

He wasn't sure when the idea had first come to him. But there was no denying that Olivia had been a thorn in his flesh since she'd arrived on his doorstep, blurting out her plans to wreck Maria's marriage.

His immediate impulse had been to kick Jeremy out of his house into well-deserved oblivion and tell Maria everything, but more rational thought convinced him that he should not be the catalyst in the destruction of his cousin's relationship.

For reasons best known to himself—reasons he couldn't fathom—she seemed determined to hang in there. She wanted to make the marriage work somehow—even at a distance. And he had to respect her decision, and her needs, even if he disagreed profoundly with them.

The last time they'd talked on the telephone she'd sounded more hopeful—even chirpy. He wasn't going to be the one to bring that defeated note back into her voice.

What he hadn't allowed for was Olivia's stubborn determination to have Jeremy herself.

Indeed, he found it well-nigh incredible that someone as basically worthless as Jeremy should have two women desperate to spend their lives with him.

Either he has hidden qualities I know nothing about or he's one hell of a stud, he thought cynically.

Or was it simply that Jeremy was Olivia's first love, and she'd elevated him on to some kind of pedestal?

Whatever, it was clear that all was not perfect in the Garden of Eden, so he'd see what a little concentrated

temptation could do. Find out if he could lead Olivia astray.
Beguile her into falling in love a little.

He'd be doing her a favour, after all, because he couldn't
see any future for her with Jeremy, even if Maria gave up
the struggle and divorced him.

And he wouldn't do any lasting damage, he told himself
defensively as he stripped off his clothes.

All the same, a persistent image of her—the vulnerable
slant of her neck and shoulders as she'd sat in front of that
damned computer—kept coming into his mind. Haunting
him, he realised without pleasure.

And as he turned the shower jet on full he knew it would
be a long time before he felt clean again.

Fool. Raving idiot. Crazy woman, Olivia apostrophised herself as she carefully applied a coating of mascara to her
lashes.

She still couldn't believe she was actually doing this—
dressing to go out to dinner with Declan Malone. It must
have been shock, she decided, as she replaced the mascara
wand in its tube. Because she'd never really thought he'd
agree to stop hassling her about Jeremy. Nor could she
fathom why he'd given up so easily.

Yes, she'd located a missing file, but that could hardly
account for such an extravagant show of gratitude. Particularly when, only a few hours ago, he'd given the impression he wanted to wring her neck.

Ah, well, she shrugged. Mine not to reason why. And
it's a meal, after all.

It was also better than sitting around hoping Jeremy
would call, but she wasn't going to think about that now.

She stood back, examining herself in the mirror, adjust-
ing the fit of her black dress over her hips. It was one of
her favourites, sleeveless and square-necked, cut straight
and slim to mid-calf, and fastened all the way down the
front by large mother-of-pearl buttons. Over it she was
wearing a grey linen hip-length jacket.

Fashionably drab, she thought critically, adding a soft pink lustre to her lips.

Declan's brisk knock at the door was punctual to the second.

For a moment she was tempted not to answer. To hide in the kitchen till he'd gone. But common sense told her that he'd only go and get a key from Sasha, and she'd no wish to suffer the humiliation of being discovered cringing in a corner.

So, she pinned on a resolute smile and threw open the door. 'Good evening.'

'Good evening yourself.' Declan handed her the flowers he was carrying—twelve pink roses, wrapped in Cellophane and decorated with trailing ribbons. 'A small peace offering,' he murmured. 'To ensure the armistice holds.'

'Oh.' To her annoyance, Olivia realised she was blushing. She ducked her head swiftly, inhaling the sweet, subtle fragrance. 'Thank you. I—I'll put them in water.'

'The florist said to fill the sink and give them a good soaking.' He came in, closing the door behind him. 'Arrange them later.'

He seemed very relaxed, and completely at home, she thought with slight vexation, as she dashed to the kitchen.

He was no taller than Jeremy, and certainly not as heavily built, yet his presence diminished the room, somehow—overpowered it.

He was wearing dark grey pants and a pale blue shirt, open at the neck, the sleeves turned casually back over his forearms, and he carried a thin tweed jacket slung over one shoulder. Under the overhead light, his dark hair gleamed like living silk.

Olivia took in these details with one swift look as she came back, and felt something clench painfully inside her.

'I thought we'd go to an Italian place I know,' Declan said, ushering her up the outside steps. 'Do you like Italian food? Because if not...'

'No, I love it,' she assured him.

He lifted a hand, and a cruising cab glided respectfully to a halt beside them.

'Heavens,' Olivia said. 'Is life always as easy as that for you?'

'No.' Declan opened the taxi door for her to get in. 'I had to ask you three times to have dinner—remember?'

She sat down as far into the corner as she could get, smoothing her skirt decorously over her knees as he took his place beside her.

She said, 'I didn't think you meant it.'

'You saved my life today. Was I supposed to take it for granted?'

'I didn't do that much,' she said awkwardly. 'The technician would have done as well.'

'When he showed up,' he agreed. 'But you were in place, and you stepped in.'

He paused. 'And I gave you a hard time too. It was particularly dumb of me not to have backed up the disk, and I didn't like being reminded of my own stupidity. I'm sorry.'

'Gratitude one minute—apologies another.' Olivia shook her head in mock wonder. 'What next, I ask myself?'

He said slowly, 'I'd say—whatever we both happen to want.'

The words seemed to hang in the air between them. Startled, Olivia risked a swift sideways glance, but he was leaning back in his own corner, his face in shadow so that she couldn't see his expression.

But he seemed to be implying that a greater intimacy might be forged between them, and that was ridiculous. Impossible.

When he spoke again, his voice was casually friendly again, so maybe she was being over-imaginative. 'The guy who owns this restaurant is from Venice. Have you ever been there?'

'Once. A schoolfriend and I went for a weekend city

break. Our parents arranged it as a reward for passing our
A levels.' She laughed. 'That was a long time ago.'

'Maybe it's time you paid another visit.'

'Yes, I should.' It would make a wonderful place for a
honeymoon, she thought, with sudden dreaminess.

'But a rather more romantic one, perhaps,' he added silkily, as if he'd picked up what she was thinking.

Olivia bit her lip. Memo to self: Stop being so transparent, she muttered silently. You're dealing with an expert
on mind-probing here.

The restaurant was tucked away in a side-street. It con-
sisted of several inter-connected rooms with tiled floors,
lamplit tables covered in crisp white linen and lots of green
plants in wall brackets. The proprietor's wife greeted them
with smiling warmth, before conducting them to a secluded
table for two.

There were a number of people already seated, and
Olivia was uncomfortably aware of a stir of interest as they
passed and Declan was recognised.

She could tell by the reactions of the women that their
stares and whispered comments weren't purely on the
grounds of his celebrity status, but because he was a dy-
namically attractive man. Sexual charisma by the cartload.

She felt conscious, as she registered the curious looks
that came her way too, that she was wearing a department
store dress and jacket rather than a designer outfit.

I don't fit the image at all, she thought with a mental
shrug. But, after all, it's only for one evening. It's not as
if I'll be seeing him again... And paused right there as
something dangerously like a flicker of regret came and
went in her head.

She was glad to sit down and bury her rather flushed
face in the menu.

'Any particular likes or dislikes?' Declan smiled at her.

'Not really.' Her nose was twitching at the aroma of
garlic, wine and herbs hanging evocatively in the air. 'I've
just realised I'm starving,' she confessed.

'You mean you're not on some diet which cuts out all that makes life worth living?' Declan raised his brows in mock astonishment. 'My God, this promises to be a night to remember. Shall we go for it?'

'Why not?' She returned his grin with a touch of uncertainty. The temptation to relax—go with the flow—was almost overwhelming. Almost. Yet a warning voice was whispering in her ear, Take care.

They made their choice, and a bottle of ice-cold Frascati was brought to the table together with some mineral water.

'So,' Declan said when the waiter had withdrawn, 'what shall we drink to?'

'Happiness?' Olivia suggested with a hint of challenge.

'Happiness,' he echoed mockingly. 'Whatever form it takes,' he added, touching his glass to hers.

Olivia wasn't sure that was what she'd meant at all, but decided not to contest the point. At least, not on an empty stomach, she thought, as the crisp wine caressed her throat.

'And are you happy?' he asked. 'In London, I mean?' he went on, as Olivia gave him a sharp look.

'I expect I'll get used to it in time. Although I haven't really seen much of it yet.'

'People who live here rarely do,' he said. 'They seem to stick very much to their own communities.'

Olivia shook her head. 'That won't do for me. I want to go everywhere—Buckingham Palace, Madame Tussaud's, the Zoo, the Tower—' She broke off, grimacing. 'I suppose that's very uncool.'

'And incredibly refreshing.' There was an odd note in his voice, and he was frowning slightly. He paused. 'Tell me, how do you come to know so much about computers?'

'That was my job in Bristol. I did on-site training in offices—one to one and in groups. You have to come up with the answers pretty quickly in that situation.'

'I see.' His frown deepened. 'And now you find yourself temping?'

'Yes.' Olivia lifted her chin. 'Is there something wrong with that?'

'You tell me.' He passed her the dish of black olives which had been placed on the table with a basket of bread. 'It seems to me you gave up a hell of a lot to come here.'

'Clearly I thought it was worth it.' She gave him a level look.

'Indeed.' There seemed to be a sardonic twist to his mouth, or was it just a trick of the light? She couldn't be sure. 'I hope you continue to think so.'

'What does that mean?' She stiffened.

'I mean when you've finished all your sightseeing, and the novelty's worn off, and you have to settle down to being just another commuter.' He drank some of his wine. 'And I think the evening might go better if you stopped looking for ulterior motives in my every utterance,' he added drily.

'Does that mean there aren't any?' Olivia raised her brows.

'Certainly not,' he drawled, and laughed out loud at the suddenly arrested expression on her face. 'For one thing, I've been commissioned to make sure you continue to work for us. I gather you have doubts. I'm supposed to charm them away.'

'I can't think why you should want to.'

'Because you're sweet-tempered, decorative, and a pleasure to have about the place,' Declan said promptly, startling an unwilling laugh from her in turn. 'You also seem to know Scriptec inside out, which makes you almost unique and definitely irreplaceable.' He paused. 'I might lose another file tomorrow.'

Olivia shook her head. 'I don't think so. And you have the Hogarth technician to fall back on.'

'Ah,' he said softly, the silvery eyes glinting at her. 'But I'd much prefer to fall back on you.'

'And there are software programs coming out all the time which locate missing stuff on the hard drive,' Olivia went on, trying to ignore the fact that she was blushing again. 'FailSafe is supposed to be good. I suggest you consider it.' She paused. 'So much less trouble than a human being.'

'I'm really beginning to think so. However, I tend to leave the technical details to other people,' he said, with a touch of dryness. 'I've learned basic skills, but I'm not a lover of machines.'

'But you work in a high-tech media,' Olivia objected.

'Because I'm obliged to. Left to myself, I'd probably be stuck in my garret, using a quill pen.'

'Some garret.' She smiled reluctantly as their first course arrived.

They'd chosen *bruschetta*—toasted wedges of garlic bread, some thick with pâté, others with a delicious mix of tomatoes, olives and olive oil.

'Wow,' Olivia said as she took the first bite. 'This packs quite a punch.'

'Don't worry,' Declan said soothingly. 'Garlic's fine as long as you both have some. I mention it for future reference only,' he added swiftly as her brows snapped together. 'Maybe you'll come here with Jeremy.'

'I thought we'd agreed not to mention him.'

'A slip of the tongue.' His voice was smooth. 'Forgive me, and let's concentrate on our food.'

That was easily done. They finished off the Frascati with the black linguine and scallops which followed, and drank Chianti with their main course of venison, served with a sharp cherry sauce.

They talked over the meal, avoiding vexed topics, Declan keeping her amused with stories of the famous and the infamous that he'd encountered during his journalistic career, and encouraging her to talk about herself too—asking her about her family, her childhood, all her early hopes and dreams.

And Olivia, forgetting that he was one of television's most skilled interrogators, responded happily.

ing in sudden sharp delight which only ended when he
lifted his head and stepped back.

'God bless convention,' he murmured. 'Sleep tight,
Olivia.'

Hand pressed to her burning lips, heart drumming un-
evenly against her ribs, she watched him walk away down
the street. And could only be thankful he would never have
the least idea how desperately she wanted to call him back.

CHAPTER SEVEN

THE alarm shrilled and Olivia turned wearily over, punching it into silence. She lay back on her pillow, arms folded behind her head, and stared up at the ceiling.

'What a mess,' she said aloud. 'What an unholy, boiling mess.'

How long could it be before Jeremy knew that she'd not only been out to dinner with another man, but stood in a London street and allowed him to kiss her? And not a peck on the cheek either, she thought dismally. But the real thing.

Declan was probably telling him now, over the cereal and croissants. Always supposing he hadn't woken him the night before with the glad tidings. She suppressed a groan.

Oh, she'd seen the trap. She'd been on edge all evening. But she'd walked into it just the same.

You could be deeply, sincerely in love with someone, but that didn't mean lust was off the agenda. Someone had told her that a long time ago, but she'd never believed it until now.

And that was all she felt for Declan, she told herself with emphasis. Simple, old-fashioned lust.

After all, she reasoned, he was attractive, successful, and powerful—a heady mixture of aphrodisiacs indeed. He'd fed her wonderful food and paid her special attention. He might even have flirted with her a little, she thought uncertainly. Anyway, he'd done everything right.

Except that he wasn't Jeremy—and he should have been. Because that was the kind of evening she'd wanted—longed for—when Jeremy had taken her out, instead of the fiasco that had actually ensued.

So how could it be that Declan, a stranger, seemed to know almost by instinct what she would like?

More experience, she thought, wrinkling her nose as she remembered the redhead in the towel and the blonde in the restaurant. There was probably little he didn't know about pleasing women—in every way.

Looking back, she supposed that she'd wanted him to be Jeremy so much that somehow some of the feelings she'd been experiencing—her confusion, loneliness and need—had been transferred to him.

That was the only excuse she could make, and pretty pathetic it was too.

Because, in truth, there was no valid excuse.

And if Jeremy was furious with her, she would have no one to blame but herself.

She pushed back the covers and trailed into the kitchen to put the kettle on, only to be confronted by Declan's pink roses waiting for attention.

She groaned inwardly. She ought not to keep them, she thought, touching one delicate bud with a tentative forefinger. They were a dangerous reminder of something best forgotten. But they were just too lovely to throw away.

While waiting for the kettle to boil, she cut the stems and arranged the roses in a jug she found in one of the cupboards.

She showered and dressed casually in jeans and a sweatshirt. She'd just finished breakfast when Sasha tapped on the door.

'Hello, darling. I just wanted to tell you that I've decided to have those panic buttons installed, and someone will be calling this afternoon. I don't think women living on their own can be too careful.'

'Sasha—please don't go to extra expense on my account. I'm not nervous—really.' Olivia spoke awkwardly. After all, she thought, she wouldn't be staying here much longer. She'd either be moving in with Jeremy or going back to Bristol to lick her wounds.

'It's just a precaution. I'm sure we'll never need them.' Sasha's gaze alighted on the jug of roses. 'Darling—how beautiful. Pink roses.' She sent Olivia a shrewd glance. 'You have an admirer.'

'Heavens, no.' Olivia forced a laugh. 'They're just a thank-you gift. I—I did someone a favour.'

'The first flowers I ever received from my beloved were pink roses.' Sasha spoke softly, her bright eyes glinting with sudden moisture. 'He said that crimson roses were the flowers of passion, but pink blooms meant true love that would last for ever. And so it was with us,' she added with a sigh.

'In this case, I imagine they were the last bunch left in the shop,' Olivia said crisply.

Sasha tutted reproachfully. 'How very unromantic, darling. Anyway, I came to say that if you're out this afternoon, I'll let the workman in.'

After Sasha had flitted away, Olivia found herself wondering again who the 'beloved' she referred to had been.

I must ask Declan, she thought idly, then stiffened. What am I talking about? That's the last thing I need. No more cosy chats under any circumstances.

It shocked her to realise how much personal information he'd extracted from her the night before—as if he was compiling a dossier, she thought darkly.

But she wasn't going to hang about brooding. It was another fine day and she was going to take some time off, start her sightseeing programme with a ride on one of those open-top buses. Apart from anything else, it might clear her head, she acknowledged with a sigh. Help her to decide what to do next in her working life.

She left her mobile phone behind quite deliberately. She'd deal with any messages when she returned, but while she was out she wanted no interruptions or hassle. Just a few hours totally to herself.

She shared the upper deck on her bus with a party of eager Japanese tourists, commingled with some Americans and a number of Australians too, feeling self-conscious because she wasn't festooned with the latest camera equipment.

But she enjoyed the trip round various famous landmarks, and her subsequent stroll along the Embankment. She found a pub offering hot roast beef sandwiches, and accompanied them with a glass of the house red wine.

Then she caught a bus to Oxford Street, and spent an agreeable hour or two exploring the big department stores, planning the clothes she would buy when she was earning regularly, and testing scents and cosmetics. In the end the only purchase which tempted her was a slice of game pie and a selection of salads from one of the food halls, which took care of supper.

When she arrived back at Lancey Terrace, she found the security firm's van parked outside, so she walked on to the gate into the garden and let herself in.

The afternoon sun was warm on her back, but there was a hint of crispness in the air, suggesting that autumn was waiting.

Not that she minded. It would be good to see the back of humid, airless nights, and besides, autumn had always represented a time of new beginnings for her. School and college years started then. It was her birthday the weekend after next, and it had been September when she'd met Jeremy again.

Almost without being aware of it, she followed the path that Humph had taken the other day, and found herself in the little clearing with the sundial. She sat down on the bench, depositing her carrier bag at her feet, and flexing her toes inside her simple navy slip-ons.

It was very quiet in the garden today. She could barely hear the incessant traffic, and most of the residents who lived around it would be at work, of course.

As I should really have been, she reminded herself, with a touch of guilt.

She still hadn't come to any firm decision about what to

do. Common sense told her that the job at Academy Productions was probably the best offer she'd get for a long time. But female instinct warned her to think again.

There was no disguising the fact that she found Declan disturbing. She'd been concerned to discover how many times he'd slipped insidiously into her mind that day. How many times she'd found herself wanting to share something with him—a thought—even a wry grin about her fellow tourists, and their determination to film every inch of their route.

She remembered almost breathlessly how his silvery eyes sparked with amusement—the way his mouth slanted into a smile. He'd been smiling when he bent to kiss her. She was sure of it.

In contrast, it was even more worrying that she'd barely thought of Jeremy at all. And yet he ought to have been her chief concern.

I should be going quietly out of my mind, she thought, frowning at the sundial. Wondering what Declan's told him. Figuring out if and how I can repair the damage.

Instead, she felt remarkably calm.

She couldn't pretend that she and Jeremy had enjoyed the ideal relationship since she'd arrived in London. Maybe she'd pitched her expectations too high, and bad beginnings didn't necessarily preclude happy endings, she told herself emphatically.

He's changed since we've been apart, she thought restively. He used to be so tender and gentle when we saw each other. So full of plans. Always talking about how it would be when we could be together.

Even when he knew he was moving to London...

That could have been Beth speaking, Olivia thought, biting her lip. Coming from herself, it was arrant disloyalty. Naturally he wouldn't discuss his plans while they were still in the melting pot. Although she couldn't deny it had been a shock when he broke the news.

Anyway, distancing himself from Bristol and all its associations should have made things easier. But that was before he'd complicated matters by moving in with Maria's cousin, she reminded herself with a touch of bitterness. And before she'd messed things up further by renting a flat just round the corner.

In Bristol, it had been difficult to see each other as often as they'd wanted, she thought defensively. Most of their meetings had been stolen, and far too brief, although they'd spoken on the phone nearly every day. She just hadn't expected those difficulties to follow them to London. That was why she felt so disappointed and—restless.

We need to sit down together and talk, she thought. Not in a crowded pub, when he's waiting to dash off somewhere—or a trendy restaurant, where we can't hear ourselves think—or even in the flat, where we could be interrupted at any moment.

She looked round the clearing. This would be the ideal place. Secluded, hidden, and so peaceful. She'd sit in the circle of his arm, her head on his shoulder, and they'd make their plans all over again. Recapture the old magic.

They said wishing could make it so, she thought wistfully. And maybe it could be true.

Olivia closed her eyes, letting the warmth of the sun play on her lids, trying to conjure up an image of Jeremy as he'd been only a few months ago, smiling at her, telling her that she was the only girl in the world for him.

She tried to capture him in her mind's eye, but he was elusive, and she couldn't see him clearly. But she felt that he was close, just ahead of her down some sunlit path, and all she had to do was follow. Follow...

Only the golden glow of the sun was in her eyes, dazzling her, and she couldn't find him anywhere.

And then suddenly she was back in the clearing, and Jeremy was beside her just as she'd wanted, making her feel so safe—so secure.

She felt his hand—or perhaps his lips—brush her hair, and she smiled, and said, 'I love you.' And forced open her heavy eyelids so that she could see him at last. Fill her heart with him as he affirmed his love for her in turn.

Only he wasn't there, she discovered with a start. Instead she was confronted by Declan, sitting at the other end of the bench, watching her.

Olivia shot upright, uneasily aware that she had a crick in her neck.

'You?' she queried dazedly, pushing her hair back from her face. 'What are you doing here?'

'I'm a resident—remember? I live just over there.' He pointed. 'So I'm allowed to be here.'

'I meant when did you get here?' She shook her head. 'I didn't hear you...'

'You're telling me.' He sounded amused. 'You were out for the count.'

'Oh.' She gave him a suspicious look as she rubbed her neck. He would be the one to find her snoozing in the sun, she thought savagely, head thrown back and mouth, no doubt, wide open. 'Was I snoring?'

'Just purring a little.' His voice was solemn, but his eyes were dancing. 'It must have been a beautiful dream.'

She flushed. 'I—I don't remember.' She paused. 'Why didn't you wake me?'

'Because you looked so peaceful. And so relaxed too, for a change. I didn't want to see you snap back into uptight mode.'

It was disturbing to contemplate that he'd been sitting there, watching her, and she'd been totally unconscious of it. She wondered how long he'd been there, suspecting that her face was red and her appearance generally dishevelled. She also hoped that she didn't talk in her sleep...

She bit her lip. 'Haven't you been at work today?'

'Indeed I have—spending a lot of time trying to contact you through your agency. When they couldn't reach you, I thought I'd try the personal approach. But when I called at the flat Sasha said she'd spotted you heading for the garden.' He spread his hands. 'So here I am.'

'My God,' she said. 'It's like being in the village at home. Their grapevine has the Internet beaten to a pulp. I thought Londoners minded their own business.'

'But I'm not a Londoner,' he said. 'I'm Irish, just passing through. And everyone in my own village takes a healthy interest in each other's affairs too.'

'But how did you know I'd be here in this particular spot?' She shook her head. 'I thought no one ever came here. That I'd have it to myself.'

'Dream on, Olivia.' His voice was sardonic. 'It's a favourite thinking place of mine too.'

'Oh.' She was silent for a moment, digesting this. Realising with chagrin that her sanctuary was nothing of the kind. More of a minefield, in fact. She decided to go on the offensive. 'Why are you trailing me like this?'

'Because we've made you a job offer and we'd like an answer as soon as possible.' His tone was matter-of-fact.

'And supposing I haven't made a decision yet?' She lifted her chin.

'Then any time in the next twenty-four hours will do. No pressure, of course,' he added laconically.

In spite of herself, she felt her mouth twitch into a reluctant grin.

'Even if I'm going to say no?'

'Now why should you do a stupid thing like that?'

'An instinct for self-preservation, perhaps?' she suggested drily.

'And what makes you feel you need to preserve yourself?' His voice suggested mild interest only.

'Any number of things.' She swallowed. 'I—I shouldn't have had dinner with you last night.'

'Didn't you like the food?'

'It was—wonderful.' She stared rigidly at her hands, tightly clasped in her lap. 'But that's not it. I had no right to accept your invitation—get myself into that situation.'

'Well, don't worry it,' he said soothingly. 'I promise I won't make it an obligatory clause in your contract.'

She gave him a level look. 'That isn't what I mean, and you know it.'

'Why, Olivia,' he said mockingly. 'Surely you're not coming all nineteenth-century over a goodnight kiss. It's just a small social convention after all.'

'Oh,' she said. 'Is that what you call it?'

'Yes,' he said softly. 'And I'm sorry to my heart if you read more into it than that.'

'It was hardly,' she said, 'a peck on the cheek.'

'No,' he agreed. 'But at the same time it's a world away from the way I'd kiss you if I seriously meant to make love to you.'

He paused, and Olivia, suddenly breathless, felt the silence tingle along her nerve-endings.

'And if you don't believe me,' he added gently, the silvery eyes lingering on her parted lips, 'you could always move closer and allow me to show you.'

She swallowed past her dry throat, her gaze fixed on him as if she was mesmerised. Because, she thought numbly, it would take so little to do as he said. To go into his arms, and taste his mouth on hers again. To feel his hands exploring her bare skin, the long fingers divining all her most intimate secrets, coaxing her to some unguessed-at edge of pleasure.

'After all,' he went on, more briskly, 'the sun's warm, the grass is dry, and I've nothing planned for the next hour or so. How about you?'

She gasped, finding sanity and speech in the same second. 'Are you mad? How—how dare you?'

Declan laughed. 'I dare because when you take on that prim look, the temptation to tease you a little is quite irresistible.'

'So, perhaps you understand why I don't want to work for you.' Her voice shook.

'Oh, you'd be much safer at work,' he said. 'There it's construed as sexual harassment, and it involves tribunals and hefty compensation. We all avoid that stuff like the plague.'

Olivia bit her lip again, aware that he was still winding her up.

She said quietly, 'I notice you haven't mentioned Jeremy. He might have an opinion about my working for you.'

'And, presumably, about my taking you to dinner?' He shot her an amused glance.

'Possibly.' Her heart was suddenly hammering again.

'Then why tell him?' He sounded totally reasonable. 'After all, it was hardly a heavy date. And I meant what I said, Olivia. The truce still stands. I'm not out to make trouble for you.'

Her immediate reaction was one of relief. Yet here she was again—involved with Declan in another conspiracy of silence. And that couldn't be right. But she'd worry about that later.

She said, 'I still don't think accepting Academy's offer would be wise.'

'No,' he said. 'You're probably quite right. After all, you have your future all mapped out. You don't need a real job. And Jeremy's already had one career woman in his life, so I doubt he'd be keen to take on another. He finds success in others a little swamping.'

He nodded reflectively. 'I can see it would be far better for you to stick to temping. Not nearly so risky.'

Olivia stared at him. 'That's ridiculous,' she objected heatedly. 'It's also unfair, untrue, and not what I meant either. And Jeremy would be delighted if I got a decent job,' she added defiantly.

'I bow to your superior knowledge,' Declan said with a faint shrug. 'Then what's the problem?'

I am, she thought wretchedly. Because I don't trust myself when you're near me. I don't trust my reactions. You make me feel as if I'm being unfaithful to Jeremy, and it worries me.

Head bent, she said, 'I suppose—it's an instinctive thing...'

He sighed. 'Olivia, listen to your head rather than your heart. You need a well-paid job. We need a trouble-shooter—someone who can teach the secretarial staff how to use Scriptec properly.'

'But that wouldn't take all my time,' she objected.

'No, but you won't be idle,' he said drily. 'You'll be taking over Kim's duties while she's on maternity leave—providing clerical support, researching programme material. God, the list is endless.' His mouth twisted. 'I can promise you won't be bored.'

No, she thought. That's what I'm afraid of.

'Would you like me to clear it with Jeremy for you? Make sure he has no serious objections?'

The faint note of mockery she detected needled her.

'I don't need his permission,' she said tautly. 'Or anyone's.'

'Then you'll take the job?'

She hesitated, then gave a curt nod.

'Good,' he said crisply. 'Then we'll expect you back on Monday. We'll make all the arrangements with the agency, and pay their commission. I hope that's satisfactory?'

'Yes,' she said. 'Thank you.'

He got lithely to his feet. 'Then I'll go, and leave you to your repose.'

'I think I've slept enough,' Olivia said with asperity. 'It seems to have addled my brain.' She got to her feet too, reaching down for her carrier. 'There's just one thing—who do I report to on Monday?'

'Kim worked for me.' He smiled at her, the silvery eyes glinting. 'Did I forget to mention it?'

And was gone.

The agency had phoned twice during the day, Olivia discovered when she got back to her flat. And there was also a message from Jeremy, with a number where he could be reached after five.

Judging from the background noise, and the fact that he had to be called to the phone, Olivia decided that he must be in another pub or wine bar, and sighed inwardly.

His voice was ebullient as he greeted her. 'Hi, sweetie. How's everything going?'

'Good, I think,' she returned, more sedately. 'Actually, I've been offered a job.'

'Yes, with the temp agency. You told me.'

'No, this is slightly different—'

'Well, I hope it pays well,' he cut across her. 'Because I've been checking out flats, and the kind of thing we'll need is going to cost an arm and a leg.'

Her spirits revived slightly. 'Can we go and look at some properties—this weekend, maybe?'

'Not a chance, I'm afraid, darling. One of our big clients is sponsoring a pro-am golf tournament in the Midlands, and I have to go and show the flag—make sure it all goes smoothly.'

'Oh,' Olivia said flatly. 'Does that mean I won't be seeing you?'

'Darling, I'm completely snowed under at the office. Going back there presently to do some catching up, actually. I haven't got any real free time until next week.'

She said slowly, 'Well, couldn't I come to this golf tournament with you?'

'Livvy, you'd be bored witless. And I'm there to work, so I'd have no time to spend with you.'

Dry-mouthed, she said, 'There'd be the nights...'

'That's not guaranteed either.' His tone was brisk. 'If they want to stay up drinking until dawn, I'll have to keep with them in case of trouble.'

'Yes,' Olivia managed. 'Yes, I see.'

'Is something wrong?'

She said slowly, 'I suppose I'm a little disappointed...'

'I'm sorry, sweetheart, but the job has to take priority at the moment. And we can't spend our lives in each other's pockets. I mean we both need our space. What?' His voice became muffled. 'Yes—fine—I'm coming right now.'

He came back to her. 'Livvy—I have to run. But I'll be in touch when I get back from the golf. Treat yourself to a new dress, and I'll take you clubbing.'

After he'd rung off she sat for a while, staring sightlessly at the jug of pink rosebuds, trying to come to terms with the fact that she'd just offered herself to Jeremy and been rejected.

He probably wouldn't regard it like that, yet essentially that was what had happened, she thought numbly, and he hadn't even sounded particularly regretful.

She'd intended to tell him everything—how she'd tracked down the missing files at Academy Productions and been offered more work on the strength of it.

And how Declan had taken her out to dinner. She'd planned to treat it jokily—nice food, shame about the company—but Jeremy hadn't given her the chance. He didn't even seem interested in how she was spending her time.

That was the hurtful thing, she thought sadly. Surely he hadn't always been like this—had he?

Yet, looking back, she could remember all the hours they'd spent as he'd dissected his failing marriage, or brooded over the office politics which he'd complained were holding him back.

Not that she'd minded, she told herself with emphasis. On the contrary, she'd been glad to be there for him— happy to know she'd be able to make it all up to him—but it hadn't left a lot of time for her own day-to-day triumphs and anxieties. But then, compared with his, her career seemed a very muted thing.

Declan's words, 'He finds success in others a little swamping,' suddenly re-echoed in her mind.

I'll never be a challenge to him, she thought bleakly. Is that the attraction?

'No,' she said angrily, aloud. 'I can't believe it—and I

won't. Oh, what's happening to me? I never had all these
doubts before...'

She stopped, her throat tightening. Because she knew
exactly what was happening to her. The cause of her doubts
was six feet tall, with eyes that gleamed like silver and a
smile that had curled into her mind.

He was called Declan Malone, and from Monday she
would be spending every working day in his company.

Which could turn out to be the worst and most dangerous
decision she'd ever made in her life.

CHAPTER EIGHT

RIGHT up to the moment when she walked up to the glass door of Academy Productions and pressed the entrance buzzer, Olivia hadn't been sure she was going through with it.

That morning, she'd looked at the newly fitted panic button beside her front door and been sorely tempted to use it. Because she was panicking badly.

'Get a grip,' she adjured herself, and marched determinedly into the building.

When she arrived in Reception, she was greeted by Mimi grinning broadly. 'Welcome back,' she whispered. 'Carol's got a face like vinegar, so you must have done something right.'

'I'm not so sure about that,' Olivia returned.

She'd just hung up her jacket when Carol bustled in.

'So there you are,' she said sharply. 'Just because Declan won't be in till this afternoon does not mean you can waste time down here. I have some company administration details to go through with you, and I've already been up to your office twice.'

'I'm sorry,' Olivia returned neutrally. 'I was here for nine am.'

Carol sniffed. 'I think you'll find the real high-fliers arrive well before that. Anyway, come along; I haven't got all day.'

Olivia dutifully filled in the forms she was handed, and gave her National Insurance number.

Having the morning alone seemed like a reprieve, until Carol passed her a small cassette.

'Declan left this for you last night,' she said ungra-

ciously. 'I suggest you deal with it before he comes back.'
And went off with her paperwork.

Last night? Olivia repeated to herself, blankly. That can't
be right. She slotted the cassette into the playback machine,
and slipped on the earphones.

'I hope you're listening to this, Olivia, or I shall feel a
right eejit.' The faintly amused drawl made her feel as if
he was standing beside her. She almost glanced up to look
at him. 'I thought maybe you should read through the
scripts you salvaged—familiarise yourself with them as
we'll be working on them together. I've left some further
notes about William Pitt on this tape, which I'd like you
to add to the file.'

There was a pause. 'And before you start gnashing your
teeth and calling me names, let me say I never in this world
took it for granted that you'd be working for me. I just
hoped. See you later.'

Oh, very clever, Olivia thought savagely as she clicked
on to Scriptec. And very manipulative, too, Mr Malone.

Formality, she'd decided, was the safeguard she'd em-
ploy. She would keep the boss and secretary limits strictly
observed. Because even if Jeremy did not exist, there could
never be any personal relationship between herself and
Declan Malone. He was a media star, and she'd been behaving like the worst kind of groupie—glamoured and be-
dazzled by his charm.

And the most sensible course would be to treat it as if it
was some kind of allergy that she'd picked up, she thought
fiercely. And avoid any recurrence.

However, as she began to type the notes he'd left she
found she was becoming interested in spite of herself. History hadn't been a particular interest of hers at school, but
this series was going to be based firmly on the personalities
of its subjects, and the turbulent times they'd lived through.
She could see how that could capture viewers' imagina-
tions.

It was past midday when she finished reading the draft

scripts. As she replaced them in their folder she heard foot-
steps in the corridor outside, and Declan's voice.

She looked up, startled, as he came in, tossing a last
remark over his shoulder. He paused in the doorway, leaning against the frame, looking her over critically. 'So you
came.'

'Of course. What did you expect?'

'Oh, there are few certainties where you're concerned,
Olivia. I soon learned that.' He paused. 'What do you think
of William Pitt?'

She glanced down at the folder. 'A very complex char-
acter. It made me wonder what he might have achieved if
he hadn't died so young.'

'Not all his achievements were so great,' Declan said
caustically. 'He introduced the first ever income tax to pay
for the Napoleonic Wars.' His mouth twisted. 'Maybe
someone should tell the Treasury that Bonaparte's dead.'

He straightened. 'Anyway, get your jacket. We're going
to lunch.'

'I'd prefer to have a sandwich at my desk.'

'I'm sure you would, but it isn't a social invitation,' he
said brusquely. 'I'm having a working lunch with Matt
Hartley, who's going to produce the series. I need you to
take notes. I'll see you in Reception in five minutes.'

He turned and left.

Olivia drew a deep breath. She need not have worried
about drawing limits, she thought. Declan had done it himself in a few well-chosen words.

So, now she knew exactly where she stood, and she
should have been reassured at the very least. Instead, she
had the strange impression that she'd lost something that
was very precious to her. And that, she thought, as she
trailed downstairs to fetch her jacket, made no sense at all.

By the end of her first complete week at Academy
Productions, Olivia was beginning to feel less edgy.
Declan's behaviour continued to be impersonal and busi-

nesslike. He was not an easy taskmaster, as she'd soon discovered, expecting every request to be dealt with instantly and caustic when the results fell short of his expectations, but this had placed her on her mettle, and she took pride in ensuring he had little to complain about.

It was like an unspoken contest between them, with the preferred result an honourable draw.

She was at her desk dealing with his mail just after eight-thirty each morning, and she rarely left before six, sometimes staying much later.

As well as the series, he was preparing for the new Parliamentary session, listing possible legislation, and those politicians who'd be ready to attack or defend it.

'But that's mainly a stand-by agenda,' he'd told Olivia once. 'It's the fighting behind the scenes that interests me most. The issues they don't want to be asked about. So you offer the bait—then catch them off-guard—get them to speak outside the official parameters—say things they never intended.'

'Does that always work?' Olivia had asked doubtfully.

'No—it's like a game of chess. You have to be thinking at least three moves ahead, while they try to block you, until someone runs out of options.' He'd shaken his head. 'When it works it makes compulsive television.'

No, Olivia thought. It's you that makes it compulsive.

She'd been to the TV studios with him, and watched him in front of the camera—seen how it loved him, felt the excitement, the sense of danger he exuded. It had stirred the fine hairs on the nape of her neck and sent a shiver tingling down her spine.

Because she was working hard, it left her little time to brood over Jeremy.

He'd come back from his golf tournament, full of beans about how well it had gone, and the triumphant part he'd played in it all.

'This is going to do me no harm at all with the company,' he'd told her smugly, before embarking on an exhaustive description of the hotel they'd used as a base, and the amount of champagne that had been drunk over the weekend.

She was pleased for him, naturally. After all, the success of his career was vital for their future, as she constantly reminded herself.

But she still hadn't told him where she was working, or Declan's part in it all, and with every day that passed it became more difficult.

It wasn't altogether her fault, she told herself a touch defensively. She'd tried several times to mention her job, but Jeremy had brushed her attempts aside with a brief, 'Good for you, sweetheart.' And eventually she'd given up.

Nor could she say that the evening they'd spent visiting various nightclubs had been unmitigated pleasure either. She liked to dance, but Jeremy had seemed to prefer propping up the bar and pointing out various celebrities, whose names, frankly, meant very little to her.

'Why did we come, if we're just going to stand about all night?' she'd asked him, tugged between amusement and exasperation.

'To be seen,' he'd told her, with total seriousness.

It had been almost a relief when she could plead an early meeting at work the following morning to cut the evening short.

But this weekend would be different, she told herself with determination, because Jeremy had promised to spend her birthday doing exactly what she wanted. He'd been full of extravagant ideas, she remembered, smiling. Tickets for a top show officially sold out for months ahead but obtainable through 'connections.' A table at the newest and most fashionable restaurant—again like gold dust, he assured her. Or he could arrange, through a client of his firm, a trip in a hot air balloon, or a drive round a leading motor racing circuit in a Formula One car.

But she'd managed to persuade him that she wanted none of these things.

'I'd like a really quiet day,' she'd coaxed him. 'I haven't been on the river yet. I thought we could go down to Greenwich—or to the Tower.'

'The Tower of London?' He'd given her a look of total incredulity. 'Whatever for?'

'Because I've never been,' she'd said patiently. She'd paused. 'And I've started taking an interest in history again,' she'd added, with slight awkwardness.

'But it's the kind of thing foreign tourists do,' he'd persisted sulkily.

She'd laughed, trying to win him round. 'OK, if it will make you feel better, let's talk in French all the time we're there. And then I'll cook you a special dinner back at the flat. It'll be fun.'

They wouldn't be under scrutiny this time, she thought, with a flutter of nervous excitement, because Sasha was spending the weekend with friends in Richmond. But she'd save that piece of information as her own special surprise for him, because she wanted the evening to evolve gently—naturally.

Jeremy had shrugged. 'Well—if that's what you want,' he'd said flatly. 'I just hope to God we don't see anyone I know.'

It hadn't been the response she'd hoped for, but when it came to it she was sure he'd enter into the spirit of the thing. And on Sunday, she planned happily, maybe she could persuade him to hire a couple of horses and ride with her in the park.

At the same time she felt a little guilty, because she knew her family were disappointed that she wasn't going home for the weekend.

But she needed to spend time with Jeremy, to recapture all the old ease and understanding they'd enjoyed, and move the relationship on.

That, she thought, was the most important thing. Without the physical commitment they were only leading half a life. It was no wonder there were problems.

Perhaps when they finally belonged to each other they'd be closer mentally and emotionally too. And there'd be no room for anyone else, even in her thoughts and dreams.

When she returned from her lunch-break on Friday, most of which she'd spent food-shopping for her birthday dinner, she found a cassette on her desk from Declan, saying he'd be out for the rest of the day, and she was free to go once she'd dealt with the material on the tape.

Brilliant, Olivia thought joyfully. She'd planned a menu that could be prepared ahead anyway, and this would give her all the time she could possibly need.

She sped through her work, grabbed her bag and fled, ignoring a spiteful comment from Carol about switching to part-time working.

As she fitted her key into the lock there was a flurry of barking and Humph joined her, his tail wagging furiously, followed closely by Sasha.

'You're early, darling.' She held out a yellow padded envelope. 'This package came for you by messenger. Were you expecting something?'

Olivia smiled at her as she bent to stroke Humph, who was frisking round her legs. 'No, but it's my birthday tomorrow. Maybe that's got something to do with it.'

'Oh, how exciting. I love birthday surprises. My beloved was so good at them.' Sasha clapped her hands. 'Do open it, darling.'

Laughing, Olivia obeyed, extracting a beribboned box of Belgian chocolates, and a card bearing a reproduction of Van Gogh's *Sunflowers*.

Sweetheart,
Sorry I can't be with you tomorrow, but Tom's off sick and I'm being sent to a conference in Edinburgh in his place. Just one of those things, I guess. Have a wonderful time, anyway.

With love, Jeremy

'What beautiful chocolates,' Sasha enthused, then, her voice sharpening, 'Olivia, are you all right? You look quite ill.'

'No.' Olivia grabbed frantically at her control. 'I'm fine—really. I—I'd made some plans, you see, which aren't going to happen after all. I'm a bit disappointed.'

'You look totally shattered,' Sasha told her candidly. 'Let me make you some coffee with a lot of brandy in it.'

'I'm not ill,' Olivia assured her. She pinned on a smile. 'Just making a fuss about nothing.'

'Hmm.' Sasha gave her a dubious look. 'Well, if you say so, of course.'

When the older woman had pattered back to her own premises, Olivia took the lid off the dustbin and dropped the chocolates and the card inside, following them up with the bags of food she'd chosen so happily.

Her eyes were burning and her throat hurt. She should have agreed to the balloon ascent, or the trendy restaurant, she thought bitterly. Then she wouldn't be spending the weekend alone.

And how strange—and how telling—that she didn't believe Jeremy had been forced into this conference at all. It was simply a useful excuse for him to seize on.

And chocolates too—the world's most impersonal gift. As if she was one of his damned clients, instead of the girl he claimed to love.

She let herself into her flat and curled up in a corner of the sofa, arms wrapped round her body.

She could always go home, but her mother for one would want to know the reason for her change of plan. She hadn't mentioned Jeremy by name, of course, but they knew that a man was involved in her decision to stay in London for her birthday, and had been clearly intrigued. So she did not feel she could face the kindly but searching inquisition which would follow if she arrived on the doorstep after all.

Besides, it might also seem a tacit suggestion that they

were somehow second-best, and she would never hurt them like that.

No, if anyone had to be hurt, it must be herself alone, she thought, as anger and disillusionment twisted inside her.

And it was perhaps a good thing that she was growing used to her own company, because it seemed, unhappily, as if she would be enjoying a lot more of it in future.

Declan felt a touch of weariness as he let himself into the house. It had been one hell of a week—for all kinds of reasons, he thought grimly. He needed a shower, and a drink—and then he had some very hard thinking to do.

As he put down his briefcase he heard a noise from upstairs, and Jeremy came into view carrying a travel bag. He checked when he saw Declan.

'Oh, hi,' he said with studied nonchalance. 'I didn't expect to see you.'

'No one ever seems to,' Declan commented drily, studying the bag with a slight frown. 'Did you mention you were going away this weekend?'

'Last-minute decision. Hell of a lot of pressure at work, so I thought I deserved a break.' Jeremy's gaze slid away evasively.

'Going alone?'

'Alas, yes,' Jeremy's tone was airy. 'I'm afraid Maria has made other plans.'

'How unlucky.' Declan's smile did not reach his eyes. Anger was building inside him, coupled with another emotion that wasn't so easy to analyse.

'Well—see you late Sunday evening,' Jeremy said, making for the door.

'No doubt,' Declan agreed levelly. 'How's the flat-hunting going, by the way?'

'Not bad.' Jeremy gave him a surprised look. 'A number of distinct possibilities, in fact.'

'I'm glad to hear it,' Declan said softly. 'Let's make your departure sooner rather than later, shall we?'

Jeremy's face went an unbecoming red. He glared at Declan, then stalked to the door, and slammed it behind him for good measure.

Declan strode into the dining room, and splashed whisky into a tumbler. He took a swift, angry swallow, then went to stand at the French windows, staring unseeingly at the sunlit garden beyond.

No prizes for guessing the identity of that little bastard's travelling companion, he thought savagely. And he'd played right into their hands by allowing her to leave work early. If he'd known, he'd have invented tasks to keep her around until midnight.

But he should have realised, he thought without pleasure. In the past couple of days she'd gone from thoughtful and a little subdued to looking as if she was lit from within with happiness. There had to be a reason.

Oh, to hell with them both, he told himself, drinking some more whisky. They deserve each other.

And he'd been wasting time and thought on Olivia which could have been devoted to a more worthwhile cause. He'd give Claudia a call—see if she'd like to have dinner. Maybe even advise him on the redecoration of the drawing room which was due. Or something.

He went to the phone and dialled her number. She was flatteringly pleased to hear from him.

'Dinner would be wonderful.' Her voice warmed. 'But why don't you come here? I'm having some other friends over on Sunday night—just for an informal supper. I nearly rang you, but I thought you'd probably be busy.'

'I have been,' Declan said lightly. 'Now I'm looking for some serious relaxation.'

'Oh.' She paused. 'Well, I'll be delighted to help—if you think I can.'

'I can guarantee the possibility,' Declan promised gravely.

He was smiling wryly as he replaced the receiver. If he was any judge, she'd be burning up her phone line for the rest of the day, trying to round up some unsuspecting souls for supper on Sunday night.

But so what? he thought with a shrug. She was beautiful, sexy, and exactly what he needed—for a while anyway. Because he was under no illusion that she was the other half of him—the woman he needed to complete his life.

And what he didn't understand, he brooded as he finished his whisky, was how he could suddenly be so sure.

The telephone rang again, and he reached for it. 'Sasha?' he queried, frowning. 'Is something wrong? Now, slow down, and start from the beginning...'

It was the most mail she'd received since she came to London, but it did little to lift Olivia's spirits. She'd cried herself to sleep the night before, and she was close to tears again as she opened the cards from family and friends in the West Country and read the loving messages, which somehow only emphasised her sense of isolation.

Her parents had sent her a bracelet of gold links, and she clasped it on to her wrist. There was a bottle of her favourite scent from her sister, and a long silky scarf patterned in grey, black and silver from her aunt and uncle too. Beth's pretty amber earrings set in silver she'd keep for a special occasion—like going home next weekend.

But, for now, she had the next forty-eight hours to get through.

Breakfast over, she went down to Portobello with a rather more sober list than that of the day before. She was becoming accustomed to the noise and bustle of the market by now, and knew exactly which shops and stalls to call at.

Her shopping soon completed, she walked unhurriedly back to Lancey Terrace. On the way, she saw that the mews house she'd noticed on her first visit was still for sale.

What a naive idiot I was, she thought, remembering the sweet, silly dream she'd indulged in.

She unpacked her provisions and put them away, then gave her surroundings a critical glance. She could always improve the day by giving the flat a thorough cleaning, she thought without enthusiasm. And she'd start by throwing away Declan's roses, now drooping wanly on their stems.

I know the feeling, she muttered inwardly, as she carried them gently to the kitchen, scattering a drift of petals behind her as she went.

The knock at the door took her totally by surprise. It couldn't be Sasha, she thought as she went to answer it, and there was no one else—unless Jeremy had decided not to go to Scotland after all...

Her throat tightened in a kind of wistful hope as she opened the door on the chain.

'Many happy returns of the day,' said Declan. 'May I come in?'

'Yes,' she said, swallowing. 'Yes, I suppose so.'

'You overwhelm me,' he murmured as he walked past her. 'I thought for a moment you were going to make me poke your present round the edge of the door.'

'You've brought me a present?' She stood looking at him in total bewilderment.

'I know it's an unusual thing to do on birthdays,' he said, 'but I'm just a born eccentric.' He handed her a small heavy parcel.

'How did you know it was my birthday?' She bit her lip. 'Sasha again?'

'No,' he said. 'You filled in some forms when you joined the company, and your personal details are now on the office database. If you're with us next year, the girls will no doubt organise the usual cake and champagne.'

'Oh,' she said. 'Well, that's hardly likely—but thank you anyway.'

'You're welcome,' he returned. 'Now you're supposed

to offer me coffee, which I sit and drink while you open your parcel.'

Her mouth trembled into a smile. 'Is that the way of it?'

'It is. And if that's your idea of an Irish accent, let me tell you it's rubbish.'

'In that case, make your own coffee,' she retorted with spirit, and he grinned and went past her into the little kitchen.

She sat down, took off the gold striped paper, and unfastened the box inside. She folded back the layers of tissue and took out the glass paperweight they'd concealed.

It was a delicate thing, a swirl of misty greys, soft pinks and silver, and at its centre, crafted in deeper pink, a tiny, perfect rosebud.

She said, 'Oh,' softly, and cradled it in her hand. She looked up as Declan came back into the room. 'I don't know what to say. It's the most beautiful thing. You shouldn't…'

'It's a bribe—to persuade you to stay at Academy and put up with my rotten temper.'

She forced a smile. 'Kim might have something to say about that.'

'Kim's going to have a baby. Her ideas may change. I'm told it happens sometimes.' He paused, then said abruptly, 'Where do you keep your coffee?'

'In the top left-hand cupboard—but I'll do it…'

'Stay where you are,' he ordered peremptorily. 'You're the birthday girl.'

'Yes, sir.' She put the paperweight gently on the table, her fingers lingering on the rounded surface.

He came back with two beakers of steaming coffee, made, she saw, as she liked it, strong with only a little milk. He must have watched the way she did it at work.

'So, what are your plans for the rest of the day?' He sat down across the table from her.

'I don't think I have any,' Olivia said, taken aback.

'You can't intend to sit here alone all day. Not on your birthday.'

She traced the pattern on the beaker with her forefinger. 'Well, originally I thought I'd go on the river—go to the Tower of London.'

'What's stopping you?'

'It was a stupid idea,' she said slowly. 'A really naff thing to do. I see that now.'

'I think it's great,' Declan said crisply. 'May I go with you?'

She looked up at him, startled. 'Why should you want to do that?'

He shrugged. 'Because, like you, I've never been to the Tower.'

'You're not serious,' she said.

'I'm going to drink this coffee,' he said, 'and then you have fifteen minutes to get ready.'

She looked down at her cream cotton pants and black rollneck sweater. 'I don't need to change.'

'No,' he said. 'But you need some make-up, or people will think I've been cruel to you, and hate me for making you cry all night.'

Colour swamped her face. She said in a suffocated voice, 'You're wrong—I haven't.'

'Don't fib.' His voice was gentle. 'And don't run away either, because I'd only come after you. You know that, don't you?'

Her lips soundlessly framed, 'Yes.'

He drank down his coffee and stood up. 'Fifteen minutes?'

Olivia nodded. Touched the paperweight. 'Thank you again for this. I shall treasure it always.'

He said quietly, 'This time I wanted to give you a rose that wouldn't wither or die. I'm glad you like it.'

When he'd gone, she picked up the weight and held its coolness against her flushed cheek for a long moment.

She said softly, 'It's my birthday—and I'm going to be happy—no matter what it costs me.'

CHAPTER NINE

IT WAS windy on the Thames, and Olivia was glad she'd put on her grey linen jacket. She unwound her new scarf from her neck and tied it over her ruffled hair, allowing the long ends to float free behind her.

Earlier, she'd applied her make-up carefully, covering the tell-tale shadows under her eyes and emphasising her cheekbones with a discreet amount of blusher. She'd sprayed herself with the Estée Lauder scent she'd received that morning, and, at the last minute, slipped Beth's amber earrings into her ears.

She thought she looked good, but if she'd been hoping for any overt appreciation from Declan she was disappointed. All she'd got was a laconic, 'Ready? Then let's go.'

They disembarked at the Tower, and walked up the ramp to join the crowds who were milling around the ticket booths and gift shop in front of the main entrance.

After her bag had been checked, they walked under the stone arch, and up the slope into the Tower itself.

Declan handed her a guidebook. 'Do you want to join a tour, or shall we just wander round by ourselves?'

'I'd rather wander.' Olivia looked up at the tall stone buildings crowding around them. She said, 'It's formidable, isn't it? Imagine being brought here, not knowing what was going to happen to you.'

'On a day like this, perhaps.' Declan lifted his face towards the sky. 'When the sun might be about to go out for ever.'

She shivered. 'That's a ghastly thought. Those were inhuman times.'

'Nothing changes very much,' he said quietly. 'These days inhumanity takes different forms, that's all.'

They walked slowly, pausing at intervals to consult the guidebook, passing the Queen's House, where Anne Boleyn and Catherine Howard had both passed their last days, and skirting Tower Green, basking innocently in the sunlight. They looked at the display of armour in the White Tower, then climbed the stairs into the Bloody Tower and saw the rooms which Sir Walter Raleigh had occupied for so long.

'He had his family in here with him for a time,' Declan told her.

Olivia wrinkled her nose. 'It's awfully cramped, and not much privacy either.'

'I don't suppose they minded—as long as they could be together.' He paused. 'Do you want to go into Martin's Tower?'

'What's there?'

'A reconstruction of the rack, among other delights.'

Olivia shuddered. 'I'll pass. But I would like to see the Crown Jewels.'

'So would half the world,' Declan said drily when they saw the queue.

'You must be so bored,' Olivia said awkwardly, as they moved slowly forward.

'On the contrary.' Declan looked around. 'I'm wondering if I can't get the company interested in another popular history series on famous prisoners who were kept here, from Henry the Sixth to Rudolph Hess, maybe.'

'I'd watch it.'

'So I should hope.' He grinned at her. 'But you're a captive audience. I've bought your loyalty.'

As the queue moved forward again Olivia was conscious that a number of curious glances were coming their way, accompanied by a lot of nudging and pointing.

She said, 'I think you've been recognised. Will your street cred ever recover?'

Declan shrugged. 'Who knows—and who cares, anyway? It's not something I allow to trouble me.'

He turned courteously as a woman came up to them shyly, proffering a postcard and a pen. 'Could I have your autograph, Mr Malone? I always watch your programme.'

'That's good to hear.' Declan smiled at her as he scribbled his signature.

'You've made her day,' Olivia whispered, as the beaming fan rejoined her party.

'I think she's started something,' he muttered back as other people began to converge on him, waving scraps of paper, as well as postcards and guidebooks. He inscribed one giggling girl's wrist, but politely declined to sign her companion's bare midriff.

'Don't you mind?' Olivia asked when they reached the comparative sanctuary of the Jewel House and began to walk round the exhibition of banqueting and church plate, displayed alongside the Swords of State and the Coronation robes.

'Sometimes, but I'm aware it's ungrateful of me.' Declan paused in front of the maces. 'They provide me with my living, and television's a fickle medium when all's said and done. It can lift you up and drop you down before you can draw breath. I plan to get out before the slide begins.'

'Oh?' Olivia looked up at him, startled. 'What will you do instead.'

'Go back to my first love—horses,' he returned promptly. 'My father always hoped I'd take over the running of our stud farm eventually, and I shan't disappoint him.'

She drew an incredulous breath. 'You mean you'd give up London? Leave your beautiful house?'

'When the time comes.' He nodded. 'To me, the secret of happiness is finding where you really belong, and doing what you know is right.'

'And for you that's horses,' she said slowly.

'Animals are honest. They'll make a welcome change to

some of the people I have to deal with.' He lifted a quizzical brow. 'Don't you think I'm capable of making the switch?'

She said quietly, 'I think you're capable of doing anything that you want.'

And they went down to the lower level to look in awed silence at the jewelled glory of the State Crowns and Coronation regalia.

'They hardly look real,' Olivia said softly.

'I'd like to have seen the original regalia,' Declan said thoughtfully. 'The stuff that Cromwell sold off or had melted down. One of the many things to curse him for.'

They emerged blinking into the sunshine, and Olivia sighed happily. 'That alone was worth the trip.' She paused. 'Thank you for bringing me,' she added stiltedly.

'It was my pleasure,' he returned. 'And I'm perfectly aware that you can make your own way back, and you don't want to take up any more of my time. But you're not getting rid of me that easily.'

'How did you know what I was going to say?' she asked indignantly.

'I've been working with you all week. I've learned to read your silences, and this one said you were figuring a tactful way of telling me to shove off.'

She choked on a giggle. 'I don't think I like being so transparent.'

'You're not,' he said. 'At least not to other people.'

While Olivia was digesting this, he went on, 'So what do you want to do after lunch—Madame Tussaud's—the Planetarium?'

She hesitated. 'Could we go to the Tate? I want to see the Turner exhibition.'

'Great idea,' he approved. 'We'll be inside when the weather changes.'

Olivia looked suspiciously at the sky, and the fluffy clouds floating in it. 'It doesn't look like rain.'

'It will be here by late afternoon, believe me. The Irish are experts on rain.'

'Well, it's very hot now.' Olivia folded her jacket over her arm. 'Would it be the pits if I had an ice-cream?'

'This is your day,' Declan said quietly. 'You can have anything that you want. Anything at all.'

She was going to joke about it being an extravagant offer, but as her eyes met his the words died suddenly on her lips, because the heated intensity in his gaze was no joking matter. His eyes were caressing her, sending a message too explicit to ignore.

She was aware of her heart hammering jerkily against her ribcage, and a strange tremor compounded of nervousness and excitement fluttering deep inside her.

She wanted to stretch out her hand and take his. To feel his arms close round her, and his mouth warm and possessive on hers.

It's because I'm hurting over Jeremy and want comfort, she told herself wildly.

But comfort was not what Declan was offering. Passion, she thought confusedly. Danger and darkness. Glory and heartbreak. All the things she dared not risk.

She turned away. 'I think lunch and the Tate are enough to be going on with.' Her voice sounded small and husky. 'Shall we go?'

She stood watching the river, forging a composure to enclose her like armour while Declan bought her ice-cream.

When he returned, her smile was self-possessed, even teasing. 'I bet it's a long time since you did that.'

'Lost in the mists of time,' he agreed. 'Take the damned thing before it melts.'

'Don't you want one?'

'I'm trying to give it up.' He leaned against the parapet, watching her with amusement. 'How old did you say you were today?'

'I didn't,' said Olivia, getting into trouble with the melting bits.

'Because you look about ten years old,' he went on. 'God, woman, you've even got some on your nose.'

'Oh, where?' She squinted, trying to see.

'Here,' he said, and bent to lick the tip of her nose, swiftly and sensuously.

For a moment the world stopped. She felt sweet, heady warmth sweep through her body. Her voice shook slightly. 'I—thought you didn't want any.'

'That's the problem with addictions,' he said. 'They can break out at any minute.'

'You're addicted to ice-cream?'

His grin slanted at her. 'Who mentioned ice-cream? Now let's go and catch our boat.'

Olivia followed, head whirling, feeling as if she stood on the brink of some dizzying abyss.

Oh, God, she thought. I've got to be so careful.

In spite of her anxieties, it was a very relaxed afternoon. They had lunch in a small French restaurant, and Olivia ate all her chicken with wine and herbs, and the *crème brulée* that followed.

She spent two enthralled hours wandering from room to room in the Tate, filling her mind with colour and light.

When they emerged, Declan's prediction had been fulfilled and a heavy cold drizzle was blowing from the river.

'Ugh.' Olivia checked at the top of the steps. 'What do we do now?'

Declan took her hand. 'We run—come on.'

Almost before she knew what was happening, Olivia found herself being whisked through enormous glass doors and into the glossy foyer of a hotel.

'Dry yourself off in the cloakroom,' Declan directed. 'I'll see you in the lounge presently.'

She found him at a table beside a large fireplace where a log fire had been lit.

'This is incredible.' She sank into the feather cushions of an enormous armchair, stretching a damp foot to the flames, as a waiter arrived with tea, a covered dish containing buttered crumpets, and a mouthwatering selection of cream cakes.

'They couldn't run to a birthday cake, I'm afraid.'

'You amaze me,' she said faintly.

'Sometimes I surprise myself.' There was an odd, almost bitter note in the quiet voice, but when Olivia looked at him, puzzled, he smiled swiftly, and passed her the crumpets.

'Declan,' she said, a while later as she refilled their cups. 'Will you tell me something?'

He gave her a guarded look. 'If I can.'

'Who is the "beloved" that Sasha mentions so often? Do you know?'

'Yes,' he said. 'Indeed I know. He was my uncle—my mother's elder brother by some years. He and my aunt had only been married for a short time when she was diagnosed with multiple sclerosis. They were unlucky, because she became very ill quite quickly, and so the marriage, as such, was over before it really began.

'He was wealthy, and he spent a small fortune on treatment for her, travelled the world looking for anything that would alleviate her condition, but ultimately it did no good, and she was confined to a wheelchair.

'It was around then that he met Sasha. He'd put some money into a West End play, and she was in the cast. By this time he was almost at the end of his tether. She saw this, and was kind to him. They became lovers, and remained so for the fifteen years that my aunt lingered. Without her, I think he'd have had a complete breakdown.'

'Did your aunt know about her?'

Declan shook his head. 'No, and she never suffered in any way because of their relationship either. My mother felt that Uncle Paul had more time for my aunt—more patience than ever before. He cared deeply, but she'd been an invalid for almost all the time they'd been together—and he was only human. With Sasha he could relax and be happy.' He gave a wry smile. 'As you must have discovered, she's got a heart as big as the world, and she was just what he needed.'

He sighed. 'When my aunt died, they planned to marry. But Sasha felt awkward about moving into the marital home, so my uncle bought the house she's living in now for them both. But he had it put in her name, and he made financial provision for her too, so that she need never work again unless she wanted.'

He shook his head. 'He was absolutely determined about it—as if he knew, somehow, that there would never be a wedding. Three weeks before it was due to take place he had a massive heart attack, and died immediately.'

'Oh, poor Sasha,' Olivia whispered. She was silent for a moment. 'So are you living in his house?'

Declan nodded. 'I was his nearest male relative, and I saw a lot of him and Sasha too, when I first came to London. He left it to me in his will.'

'Yes,' she said slowly. 'Yes, I see. It makes a lot of things much clearer.' She paused again. 'Were you fond of your aunt?'

Declan said carefully, 'She'd been a sick woman for a long time and it had made her understandably bitter. I—made allowances.'

'It's so sad,' Olivia said softly. 'Having their chance of a happy life snatched away.'

'Sasha doesn't pity herself. She has a host of friends, Humph, the occasional lodger—and her memories. She counts herself a rich woman.'

'And she has you.'

'I do what I can.'

She said carefully, 'I hope you didn't mind my asking?'

'No,' he said. 'I expect she'll tell you all about it herself, one of these days.'

'Yes.' Olivia replaced her cup in its saucer. She said, 'That was a terrific tea. In fact, the whole day's been wonderful.'

He looked at her steadily across the table. 'It doesn't have to end here. It's a big hotel, with all kinds of facilities. We could always explore a few of them.'

The words seemed to hang, charged, in the air between them.

Olivia said hurriedly, 'I don't think I'd be much of a companion.' She pantomimed a yawn. 'All that walking and food has made me sleepy.'

'The hotel also has bedrooms. Very comfortable ones, I'm told.'

No use pretending she didn't understand him now. She knew, without being told, that he'd probably made enquiries already at the desk. That if she said the word he would take her up to one of those bedrooms and make love to her, and she would yield herself to him, body and soul.

And be lost for ever.

Because there was no future with Declan. If she slept with him, she probably wouldn't have a job either. And casual sex wasn't her scene, and never had been. She believed in love. She believed in commitment, and nothing less would do.

But while Declan might well become her whole life, she would just be another telephone number on his home computer files. And eventually, as his life moved on, she would be erased—as if she had never existed at all.

She uncurled herself from the chair and got up slowly and carefully.

She made herself look at him calmly, hiding the fact that she was shaking inside, that her mouth was dry, and her legs trembling under her.

She kept her voice even and dispassionate. 'Actually, I'd prefer to go home.'

'Just as you wish.' He spoke equally coolly, showing no sign of regret. No disposition to persuade her to change her mind. He got to his feet, too, signalling to the waiter to bring the bill. 'I'll get them to call a taxi.'

Outside, it was raining heavily. Olivia scrambled into the

cab and waited for Declan to join her. But the door closed
on her alone, and she saw him hand the driver some money
after giving her address.

She opened the window. 'Don't you want a lift?'

'It's probably wiser if I walk.' His tone was ironic.

She flushed. 'But you'll be soaked.'

'On a lovely soft day like this?' he mocked. 'Never.'

The cab drew away, and through the rear window Olivia
watched him turn and walk away in the opposite direction.

It was the right thing to do, she assured herself. Absolutely the right thing. But why did it have to hurt so much?

Huddled into the corner of the cab, looking out at the glis-
tening streets and buildings, Olivia tried to make sense of
what was happening to her. The buoyant happiness which
had possessed her all day had vanished, leaving her raw
and uncertain.

Jeremy's behaviour had left her shocked and disillu-
sioned, but that wasn't sufficient cause to send her stumbling into another man's arms. And especially a man like
Declan Malone, who could have any woman he wanted—
and probably did, she thought, deliberately lacerating her
feelings.

It occurred to her that Declan had never mentioned
Jeremy's name once, or asked why she wasn't spending her
birthday with him. Yet Jeremy lived under his roof, so he
must have known exactly what his plans were.

Did he know that she'd been stood up, and had his own
invitation been issued because he felt sorry for her? Or was
there some darker motive?

Pain lanced through her at the very idea, but it had to be
faced. Recognised as a probability.

After all, seducing her would be the perfect way of ensuring that the remnants of her relationship with Jeremy
could never be rescued and restored.

And she'd nearly succumbed, beguiled by his charm and
the heady sexual charisma that surrounded him. But they

were his stock in trade, after all. They accounted for much
of his success on television. He was undoubtedly a skilled
political commentator, and a tough interviewer, but to his
female audience he was also a fantasy figure. That dangerous combination: a sexy intellectual. An object of desire.

And off I went, she derided herself, all decked out in my
new scarf and earrings, like a lamb to the slaughter.

She'd known, of course, that he held a dangerous attraction for her, but she'd believed that her feelings for Jeremy
were the barrier that would protect her from herself. But
now that relationship was faltering she realised just how
flimsy that protection had always been.

Because he was too good a companion, as she'd discovered today. She could talk to him more easily than anyone
she'd ever met. She loved his humour, and the swift, caustic
remarks which gave it an edge. She'd liked the good-
natured way he'd responded to the autograph-hunters.

Working with him hadn't helped either, she brooded. The
atmosphere in the office was high-powered—electric. She
was interested and involved—determined to match the intellectual demands he made of her. Caught up in his ef-
fortless dynamism.

And that was where it should have stopped. Out of working hours, she should have stayed totally aloof. Fought the
disloyal yearnings which tormented her. And which had so
nearly brought her to ruin.

But not again. Never again, she told herself with steely
determination.

The cabbie's bored, 'In your own time, darling,' alerted
her to the fact that she was back at Lancey Terrace.

She wouldn't wait for Jeremy to find somewhere, she
thought, as she let herself into the basement and switched
on the light. She would find herself another place to live—
as far from Declan as possible. Some of the girls at
Academy were in flat-shares, and vacancies were always
cropping up. Maybe she could move into one of them. Live

the life of a single girl, instead of depending on Jeremy for
her happiness.

And maybe he'd want her more if she wasn't quite so
readily available.

As for Declan, he knew she was alone and vulnerable
for the rest of the weekend, so that had to change. She
needed to absent herself completely in case he came prowl-
ing again, because, shamefully, she didn't know how immune she was to his particular brand of temptation.

I'll get an early train and go home for the day, she told
herself with determination, reaching for her mobile phone
to call her parents.

And if she never saw Declan again outside working
hours then surely she'd be safe—wouldn't she?

Declan slammed the front door behind him, and tossed his
keys on to the hall table. He stood for a moment, eyes
closed, a hand raking almost savagely through his dark hair
as he tried to come to terms with what he'd done.

When he'd arrived at Claudia's flat a couple of hours
earlier, his suspicions that he was the trophy guest had been
confirmed. The dinner had been superb—she was a gifted
and imaginative cook—and the wines well-chosen. The
conversation had been relaxed and enjoyable, and when the
coffee and Armagnac had been drunk the rest of the party,
well-primed, had made excuses and left them alone together.

The setting had been perfect. Claudia had left him, his
glass refilled, on the enormous sofa in her lamplit drawing
room while she said goodnight to her other guests. When
she'd rejoined him, she'd released her hair from the loose
knot she'd worn all evening, and brushed it loose on her
shoulders. In addition, she'd discreetly freshened her scent,
renewed her lipstick, and undone an extra button on her
black velvet shirt, affording him a tantalising glimpse of
the creamy curves of her breasts.

The message had been covert, but unmistakable. And

also imperative, he conceded wryly. She'd meant him to make love to her, and that had been his intention too. His sole reason for being there, in fact.

But he didn't want her. That was the ghastly, incontrovertible truth which had assaulted him. She was a lovely girl, with a sparkling personality and a delectable body, yet he'd felt—neuter. Even if she'd stripped naked, and he'd been able to tell she was considering it, her fingers casually toying with the next button on her shirt, it would have made no difference.

His body might have responded, he acknowledged ruefully. But it would have been no more than a conditioned reflex, his mind and emotions totally disengaged.

And she didn't deserve to be used. She was worth far more than that.

He had felt her puzzlement as she'd chatted, softly and huskily, watching him from under her lashes. Wondering why he didn't move closer—touch her—kiss her.

The shock in her face when he'd got abruptly to his feet, apologising, offering the lame excuse of an early-morning meeting, would haunt him, he thought grimly. Then pride, thankfully, had come to her rescue, and she'd covered well, smiling, agreeing that it was getting late, and that she had a full day coming up too.

He'd got out of the flat somehow, sparing her the insult of the casual goodnight kiss which would only have added to her deserved sense of injury.

When he'd accepted her invitation he'd known what the score was. The bargain had been made—and then, too late, he'd reneged on it.

He knew without pleasure or conceit that Claudia would be shattered—humiliated by his behaviour. What he'd done was unforgivable, and he could never excuse or explain it either to her or to himself.

What the hell's wrong with me? he demanded explosively. Am I going crazy?

He'd felt on edge, restless all day. He'd decided first

thing that he'd get out of London, and had phoned some old friends who lived near Maidenhead, inviting himself to lunch. But even a relaxed day at Charles and Tess's comfortable cluttered house, and the pleasure of playing with his young godson hadn't worked its usual miracle.

'It's time you got married and had kids of your own,' Tess had chided as he'd sat at the kitchen table, turning the business section of the *Sunday Times* into a paper hat for the baby tucked into the crook of his arm. 'Are you seeing anyone?'

'Now and then.' He'd pulled a laughing face at her.

'And is it serious?' She'd been in bulldog mode, refusing to let go.

'Maybe,' he'd returned lightly. 'I'll keep you posted.'

'I won't hold my breath.'

As he'd driven home he'd reflected that she was probably right, and that Claudia, maybe, could be the one after all. Perhaps he was a fool to wait any longer. To hope for the sudden stunning realisation that here was the woman he'd been waiting for all his life, and that he would want no other.

In these uncertain times it could be that a level of physical attraction coupled with the same interests was a safer basis for a lasting relationship.

And then he'd thought of his parents. Seen in his mind's eye his mother's shy, mischievous smile when her husband looked at her in a particular way, even after all their years together, and he had known he'd settle for nothing less.

But was that why he'd behaved like the biggest bastard in the Western world and left Claudia hurt and bewildered?

God only knows, he thought wearily. Because I don't.

He was still racked by the same feelings of uncertainty and self-disgust when he arrived, later than usual, at work the next day.

As he walked into the office, Olivia swung round from her desk and looked at him. She was pale, her eyes wide and serious, her hair dragged unbecomingly back from her face and confined at the nape of her neck by a tortoiseshell clip.

And he knew in a sudden blinding moment of self-revelation why he hadn't stayed with Claudia last night. Realised he wanted to walk across the room and pull her hair loose, lifting the soft silky strands to his lips, burying his face in the curve of her shoulder and breathing the delicate fresh scent of her skin.

And that he would want to do that for the rest of his life. Because there was no one else in the world who could fill his heart and make him complete.

The shock of it seemed to drive all the breath out of his lungs, and he found himself suddenly leaning against the frame of the door because he was shaking inside, and terrified that his legs wouldn't support him.

'Are you all right?' She was getting to her feet. If she came across the room to him he'd be lost.

'Hangover,' he lied, in a voice he barely recognised. 'Hold my calls for a bit, would you?'

The men's room was deserted. He filled the basin with cold water, splashing it across his wrists and onto his face.

When, eventually, he raised his head and looked at himself in the mirror, his face was haggard, his mouth harsh and set.

I laid the bait, he thought with anguish. I set the trap—and now I'm caught in it myself. And she doesn't give a damn about me. She's still caught up with that worthless piece of trash.

And—somehow—I have to live with that. If I can.

CHAPTER TEN

WHEN Declan did not return to the office, Olivia realised he'd gone straight into his scheduled meeting.

He must have been on one hell of a bender, because he'd looked really ill, she thought with a pang, although, admittedly, his condition didn't deserve that much sympathy.

He'd looked at her as if he didn't recognise her. Almost as if he'd forgotten she'd taken Kim's place.

She wondered if it was the aftermath of her birthday which had prompted him to drink too much. If he might have regretted his attempt at seduction and been angered by her rejection of his advances.

But she couldn't really believe that. He wouldn't take it that seriously, she told herself. He'd just shrug it off with one of his crooked grins. Phone another lady on the list.

Meanwhile she had, she hoped, got things more into perspective herself. Home was a healing place, she thought, and the rawness in her heart had been assuaged somewhat by her parents' open delight in seeing her.

She'd had to act her socks off, pretending that everything in the garden was roses, however. She'd talked brightly about her job, and the television personalities she'd already met through it. Described her flat and, with affection, Sasha, but spoken of her plans to move. And she hadn't once mentioned Declan.

'So what did you do yesterday, darling?' her mother had asked eagerly. 'Have you met someone nice?'

'No one serious,' Olivia had said, reflecting that it was no more than the truth.

After lunch, she'd gone for a long walk with the dog, so that she could think.

Firstly, she'd decided, she would have to try and put things right with Jeremy. London had obviously gone to his head a little, and she couldn't blame him for that, but when the novelty wore off, and he'd calmed down a little, she would be waiting for him, she told herself resolutely.

They both had things to forgive each other for, but maybe it would make their relationship stronger in the end.

It had all been good, positive stuff, and she only wished she could feel more cheerful about it.

As for Declan, she'd thought, biting her lip until she'd tasted blood, he was simply a charmer who enjoyed women, and there was no need to take anything that had happened between them seriously. He couldn't resist flirting, or going further if he was encouraged, and she'd be a fool to let it get to her, or allow this stupid crush on him to develop any further.

I'm no better than those autograph-hunters, she'd told herself. I need to forget the fantasy and concentrate on what's real in my life.

She'd come to work, armed with that determination, and then she'd seen Declan in the doorway, staring at her as if she were a ghost, and found herself crucified by an impulse to go to him and hold him until the nightmare in his head vanished.

Except I could be the nightmare, she realised sadly. And if it's true, I cannot bear to know.

And, on that thought, she resolved to go on to Stage B of her plan.

'You're leaving?' Sasha's voice rose in astonishment. 'But, darling, why?'

'Louise in Accounts has a flatmate who's getting married. And I'd be sharing with three others.' Olivia smiled resolutely. 'At the moment I feel a bit isolated.'

'Yes,' Sasha said distractedly. 'I can see that. But I thought... Well, never mind that. Where is this flat?'

'Wandsworth. Louise took me to see it in my lunch-hour. It's an older house, with really big rooms.'

Sasha nodded. 'When do you want to move out?'

'The wedding's in three weeks but I can move in the week before.' Olivia hesitated. 'But I don't want to leave you in the lurch.'

'You won't,' Sasha said briskly. 'Tenants come and go, and there's usually another waiting in the wings. I often think my basement is something of a rite of passage—a staging post in the search for a real life. But I didn't think you'd find yours in Wandsworth.'

'You make it sound like the Gobi Desert,' Olivia said, amused in spite of herself.

'Wait until you've lived there for a while,' Sasha said darkly. She gave a little sigh. 'Humph and I will miss you. Promise you'll keep in touch.'

'Yes, of course,' Olivia said awkwardly, not knowing if this was a promise she'd be able to keep.

When she returned to her basement, her mobile phone was ringing.

'Livvy, my sweet?'

'Oh,' she said. 'Jeremy. How was the conference?'

'Bloody dire,' he said. 'A complete disaster from beginning to end.' He spoke with enough feeling to convince her that his weekend, however he'd spent it, had not gone according to plan.

But then neither had hers.

'Did you have a good birthday?'

'Fine.' She paused. 'Thank you for your present.'

'Oh, it was nothing.'

You can say that again, Olivia thought, then kicked herself mentally. She was supposed to be building bridges here. Looking for a fresh start.

And sometimes it was better not to have too much imagination. Which was why she'd put Declan's paperweight away in a drawer.

'Listen,' he said. 'I've been neglecting you shamefully.

I suppose you've already eaten, but we could always go to a cinema. There's a new French film on that's had rave reviews,' he added eagerly. 'What do you say?'

She said gently, 'I'd love to. Where shall I meet you?'

He was really trying to make amends, she thought as she collected her jacket and bag, because he hated foreign films. Not so long ago she'd have been singing with happiness. Now, she felt quiet, and a little bleak.

But he was trying—and she would too.

It was an odd week, with Jeremy trying to second-guess her every wish, and Declan strangely remote—even taciturn. When he spoke to her it was only about work, and the atmosphere was heavy between them.

Even the news that the Prime Ministers series had definitely been commissioned by a major network couldn't lift it.

It was almost a relief when he told her abruptly that he was taking some leave, and would be away the following week.

'Are you going somewhere nice?' She tried to smile, wanting, somehow, to ease things back on the old footing. But the icy look he gave her said plainly she was wasting her time.

'I'm going to Ireland.'

And are you going alone? was what she longed to ask next, but dared not.

Instead, she said, 'I hope you have a wonderful time. You've been looking tired.'

'I'm gratified by your interest,' Declan said coldly. 'But it's quite unnecessary. And I'd appreciate being able to sign those letters I gave you before I leave tonight.'

Swine, Olivia thought hotly. Whatever his personal opinion of her, he couldn't fault her efficiency as his assistant.

She said, 'They're ready—sir,' and banged them down on the desk in front of him so hard she nearly barked her knuckles.

*   *   *

'I've found a flat,' Jeremy told her over dinner that night.

'Oh,' she said. 'That's—good.'

'Well, you might show a little more enthusiasm,' he said pettishly. 'God knows you've been harping on about it ever since you got here.'

She sighed. 'I'm sorry. Tell me where it is—everything about it.'

'It's in Notting Hill again,' he said. 'I mean—that's absolutely the in place at the moment.'

'Which is important, of course.'

'Yes, it is,' he said crossly. 'Honestly, Livvy, you have to learn about these things.'

Her hand touched the bowl of her wine glass. She remembered another rounded crystal shape, with a pink rose held for ever at its heart, and felt the breath catch in her throat.

She said, 'Maybe I feel it's more important to find where you really belong—and go there.'

'What on earth are you talking about?'

'Nothing at all. It doesn't matter.' She smiled at him. 'When are you moving?'

'Next week. The present tenant's going back to Australia for a couple of years, so I can rent until he returns, then look round for something to buy.'

'Then you'll beat me to it,' she said. 'I have another ten days before I transfer to Louise's flat.'

'Louise's flat?' Jeremy repeated. 'Darling, don't be silly. You'll be moving in with me—just as we always planned.'

A great stillness seemed to settle around her. There was an icy silence screaming inside her head.

'Livvy—didn't you hear what I said?' He was smiling triumphantly. 'We're going to be together at last.'

She found a voice from somewhere. 'Do you think that's wise?'

'What do you mean?'

'Wouldn't it be better to leave things as they are—until you're divorced anyway?'

'That could take for ever.' He reached across the table, putting his hand on hers. 'Livvy, I've been doing a lot of thinking lately, and I don't want to wait any longer.'

Olivia stared down at the table. This change of heart, she thought, seemed to stem from her birthday weekend, and his sudden absence. Something had clearly happened which had made him see her in a new and favourable light.

She would probably never know what it was, but then, she thought with a pang, she had her own secrets.

'Besides,' he went on, 'I'm rather counting on you. Do you know how much the rent is?'

'Then find someone to share with you,' she said gently. 'Advertise for a flatmate. Make sure you get references.'

'Oh, for God's sake.' He threw himself back in his chair. 'What is your problem?'

'I don't think I have one,' she said equably. 'I'm moving in with Louise, Hilary and Tricia. You're the one with the outsize rent.'

'Sometimes,' he said slowly, 'I really think I don't know you at all.'

'How could you?' she said. 'I've only recently discovered myself.' She looked at the dish of fresh peach ice-cream which had just been placed in front of her. For a brief moment she saw with total clarity the sun on the river, with the great looming bulk of the Tower in the background. And Declan laughing at her—bending forward...

Something closed in her throat, and she pushed the dish away. 'I'm not really hungry any more.'

'Leave it, then. Listen, Livvy.' Jeremy leaned forward again. 'Even if we don't live together, things don't have to go on as they are.' He laughed rather nervously. 'I mean, this celibate life is rather getting me down.'

The frozen feeling inside her deepened with the certainty that he was lying—and that it didn't matter.

'And as it happens,' he continued eagerly, 'Declan's going off to Ireland for a few days, so I'll have the house to myself.'

'Yes,' she said unguardedly, 'I know.'

He frowned. 'How do you know? Through that Sasha woman?'

'No.' She looked at him calmly. 'I work at Declan's production company—as his personal assistant.'

'What?' The word was explosive. 'Why didn't you tell me?'

'I wanted to,' she said. 'But you never seemed very interested—in my work—my wishes—anything.'

He looked at her, his eyes narrowed. 'Then I wish you luck,' he said. 'He's got a hell of a nasty tongue on him when he wants. And a temper.'

'Then I'd better stay well out of his personal territory,' Olivia returned levelly.

He said sulkily, 'Anyone would think you didn't want to be with me. You seemed keen enough once—when we never had the chance.'

She sighed. 'A lot of things have happened over the past few weeks.' She gave him a straight look. 'Maybe we both need to examine our feelings.'

Although she didn't need to, she thought, as she lay in bed that night, staring into the darkness.

She couldn't pinpoint the exact moment when she'd ceased to be in love with Jeremy. Maybe the first sense of disillusion had set in before she ever came to London, when she'd realised he'd made his plans without consulting her even marginally.

Looking back, she suspected all she'd ever felt was infatuation, triggered by her childhood memories of this golden, god-like figure.

My God, she thought. Every girl in the village was dotty about him. And when I met him again I turned him back into my girlhood fantasy. And I didn't look too closely, in case I saw something that didn't quite fit.

He even told me his wife didn't understand him, she thought, with self-derision. And I fell for it.

She could see now the future she'd planned with him had never had any substance. Jeremy didn't really want a wife, a home and all the responsibilities that went with them. He already had all that, and couldn't hack it. He'd simply told her what she'd wanted to hear, so that he could get her into bed.

And when she hadn't fallen into his hand like an apple from a tree he'd gone off to play the field elsewhere.

When he came to London, he was giving me the brush-off as well as his wife, she thought wryly. And everyone knew it but me.

It worried her that she didn't care more. She should be heartbroken—suicidal at the collapse of her dream—yet she was only sorry she'd wasted so much time and emotion on him.

Maybe that makes me as shallow and self-serving as he is, she thought, grimacing.

Except that she knew heartbreak could well be waiting for her very soon. Because recognising the truth about Jeremy had only made her see with piercing clarity what she truly felt for Declan. And it terrified her.

Because it wasn't a passing attraction. It was the kind of agonising need that could tear you apart. The kind of tenderness that could heal any wound and make you whole again. She wanted him completely—as her friend, her lover, and the father of her children. She wanted to share peace with him as well as passion, and be the one who lit the laughter in his eyes.

The barriers were down now, and she had nowhere she could hide from the truth.

That was why she'd been clinging on to the myth of her relationship with Jeremy—because it was safer than admitting the truth of her own heart.

I've found the place where I belong, she thought, and it's with Declan—at his side for ever.

Only Declan didn't feel like that, and she would have to bear the pain of that knowledge for the rest of her life. All he'd offered her, after all, was a few brief hours in a hotel room near the Embankment. And now they were strangers again—or worse than strangers.

She would almost have welcomed back the scorn and hostility of their first encounters rather than this—chilling indifference.

But the choice was not hers to make.

Some day, she thought, I won't feel like this. Some day...

But there would be many long and lonely hours to endure before it dawned.

When she arrived at work on Monday, she was waylaid by Carol.

'Don't think you're going to swan about in Declan's absence,' she said aggressively. 'It's time you started this training programme we've heard so much about.'

'Fine,' Olivia returned, and when the other woman had marched off turned to Mimi, who was flicking through a fashion magazine. 'Why is she like that? Is it something I've done?'

'Nah.' Mimi shook her head. 'It's nothing personal. Carol only likes stupid people because they make her look good. She was the same with Kim.' She paused. 'And she's jealous, of course. She's always had a thing about Declan, and when Kim got pregnant she saw it as her chance to work for him.'

'Does Declan know this?'

Mimi shrugged. 'He doesn't miss much. That's probably why she's still in Admin. He wouldn't be unkind to her, but he'd make sure he kept her at a distance. Froze her out. The last thing he wants is some PA drooling over him.'

'Oh,' Olivia said in a hollow voice. 'I see.'

She went up to the office and stood looking round her. So, she now knew the reason for Declan's cold behaviour.

He must know me better than I know myself, she thought

unhappily. But how much more can I take? Maybe it would be better to cut my losses now.

She'd spent the whole weekend, it seemed, arguing with herself, yet she still didn't know which would hurt the most—continuing to work for Declan in this new, icy formality, or leaving and never seeing him again, except as an image on the television screen.

She sat down in his chair, spreading her hands along his desk, tasting tears, thick and bitter, in her throat. Her heart felt like a frozen stone in her chest.

She found the inscription from the sundial burning in her brain. 'Love makes Time pass. Time makes Love pass.' And prayed with all her soul that it was true.

It was the longest week of her life. Olivia tried to throw herself into the simple training programme that she'd devised, but it was hard to concentrate when your heart and mind were several hundred miles away in Ireland.

She wondered if he was with the pretty blonde she'd seen in the restaurant. They looked right together, she told herself dispassionately, both of them glamorous and assured. Familiar with each other's world. Everything she herself was not.

Perhaps he'd taken her to see the alternative life that he might return to one day. To find out if she'd be prepared to share it with him.

Each evening, before she went home, she walked in the garden, drawn reluctantly to the bench near the sundial, wondering every time whether she might find Declan there. But she was always alone. No ghost lover touched her hair, or waited for her at the end of the labyrinth of her unhappy thoughts.

One night Louise took her to a wine bar to meet her fellow tenants, and she talked and laughed as if she didn't have a care in the world, determined to make a good impression. Because this was the start of the rest of her life.

On Friday morning, she was in the office dealing with

the mail when the phone rang. Her heartbeat quickened as she reached for the receiver, wondering, as always, if it might be Declan.

'Hi, Livvy.' It was Jeremy, sounding pleased with himself. 'Just to let you know I've moved into my new place.'

'You've moved already?' Olivia frowned. 'Is that what you planned?'

'It's what I've done, so what does it matter?' he said with a touch of impatience. 'And I've decided to throw a little house-warming bash tomorrow evening—eight o'clock onwards.'

'Oh.' Olivia was taken aback. 'I'm not sure...'

'Come on, my sweet, you can't let me down. It wouldn't be the same without you.' He gave a light laugh. 'After all, I want you to see what you're missing.'

Olivia obediently jotted down the address he gave her, but sighed as she put the phone down. Going to Jeremy's house-warming wasn't her idea of a fun time for all kinds of reasons, but she supposed it was marginally better than sitting at home, brooding.

She guessed Jeremy would expect a 'happy flat' present, but didn't want to take a framed print or a piece of pottery, or anything that would give out signals of permanency, so she compromised with a bottle of good champagne.

Expensive but ephemeral, she told herself wryly, as she zipped herself into a plain black dress with a low, straight-cut neckline and narrow straps, and applied a modicum of colour to her eyes and lips.

Her plan to wait until the party was in full swing, then put in a token appearance only was confirmed when she arrived at the imposing white house with its pillared portico, and met the volume of noise emanating from the first floor. The windows were open and people, she saw, had spilled out on to the balcony. Others were occupying the stairs, drinking, talking and laughing loudly, and Olivia had to edge past.

She hesitated in the doorway, looking through the crowd

for Jeremy. He was nowhere to be seen, but if the number of bodies per square foot was the criterion, his party was a wild success, she thought, grimacing inwardly.

'More supplies? Thank God.' A blonde girl with a nose-stud relieved Olivia of her champagne. 'People are leaving their jackets in the main bedroom, which is that way.' She pointed, then gave Olivia a curious look. 'I haven't seen you before. Do you work with Jerry?'

'No,' Olivia returned constrainedly. 'I'm an old friend.'

The other's grin was faintly malicious. 'Really? Maybe we should establish a support group. Anyway, dump your coat and get a glass. Most of the pouring's happening in the kitchen.'

'I'll find it.' Left alone, Olivia was tempted to beat an instant retreat, but decided she should at least greet Jeremy, and wish him good luck in his new home.

As she fought her way to the bedroom a hand grasped her arm, and, turning, she found herself looking up at Declan.

Joy seemed to explode inside her, and her mouth involuntarily curved into a smile.

'Declan? You're back.' She paused, trying to see past the cool grimness of his expression. 'I—I didn't expect to see you here.'

'I wasn't planning it either,' he said abruptly. 'I came with someone.'

Of course, she thought, her instinctive happiness at seeing him beginning to corrode into an ache of misery.

She said flatly. 'Well, if you'll excuse me, I'm on my way to find a drink.'

He said quietly, 'Olivia, do us both a favour and go. Go now.'

She tried to laugh. 'But I've only just got here.'

'It doesn't matter. It would be better all round, believe me.'

He was still holding her arm, and she pulled herself free.

'You have no right to say that. I was invited—and I'm staying.'

'Please do as I ask.' There was something like anguish in his eyes. 'I can't explain now...'

'Well, well, if it isn't the country mouse.' There was something familiar about the sultry female drawl that interrupted them. Olivia, blinking at the waft of heavy perfume assailing her, glanced round, and saw a spectacular head of red hair framing a sulky face, and a voluptuous body shown off in a minimal dress of charcoal ribbed silk. A bracelet set with lapis lazuli decorated one tanned arm.

Melinda, she thought, pain stabbing at her. The girl who'd been at Declan's house that first morning.

'So you came.' Her words were slightly slurred, but her blue eyes were hard as they swept Olivia. 'Little Miss Loser.'

Declan said harshly, 'That's enough, Melinda.'

Olivia faced her down, her chin lifted dangerously. 'You're dressed,' she said. 'Is there a shortage of bath towels?'

'Why, you...' Melinda lunged with the glass she was holding, sending the champagne flying over Olivia.

'That does it,' Declan almost snarled. 'Olivia—you're out of here.'

'No way,' she flung back at him. 'What's a little wine between friends? But I wouldn't let your girlfriend refill her glass. I'd say she's had all she can manage.'

She walked into the bedroom, slinging her jacket on to the bed with all the others and making for the bathroom so she could sponge her dress.

As she walked in she nearly tripped over the outstretched legs of a girl who was sitting on the floor, her back to the wall and her head buried in her hands.

'Oh—I'm sorry.' Olivia checked. 'I didn't realise there was anyone in here.'

The girl looked up, shaking back her dark cloud of hair. She was attractive, rather than pretty, with a strong face

marked by good bone structure now blurred and diminished
by the tears which streaked her skin and reddened her
smoky-blue eyes.

'There isn't.' Her voice was husky and shaking as she
got to her feet. 'I'm going.'

'No, please.' Olivia felt desperately awkward. 'Do use
the basin—bathe your face. I came in for some tissues because I've had a drink chucked over me.'

'We're neither of us having a very good party.' The girl
combed her hair with her fingers. 'But yours may get better.'

Olivia shook her head, remembering the way Melinda's
painted nails had closed on Declan's sleeve. The triumphant
malice glittering in her eyes. 'I don't think so.' She paused.
'Is there anything I can do to help? Do you want to tell me
what's upset you?'

'Why not?' The other laughed bitterly. 'Everyone but
you seems to know already. I came to see my husband—
we're supposed to be making a serious attempt to save our
marriage, or so I thought. And I now find he's been having
an affair all the time.' Her voice broke.

Olivia felt icy cold. Oh, God, she thought. This must be
Maria—Jeremy's wife. She looked at the pale, drawn face
and shadowed eyes, and felt a knife twist inside her.

She said, 'How—how do you know?'

'My cousin told me.' The girl ran water into the basin
and began to splash it on to her face. 'He's known about
it for a while, but he didn't say anything because he hoped
things would sort themselves out somehow.'

'And maybe they will,' Olivia said quickly. 'Perhaps it
isn't nearly as serious as you think.'

Maria shook her head. 'It's become quite blatant.
Jeremy's even invited her here tonight,' she went on, swallowing. 'Although admittedly he didn't know I'd be coming as well. Now everyone knows—and I just want to die.'

'Oh, please don't feel like this.' Wretchedly, Olivia

handed her a towel. 'I'm sure you can work something out together.'

Maria shook her head. 'Not again,' she said. 'He was seeing other women before he came to London. But he swore it had all stopped—that we'd make a fresh start. A few weeks ago he even took me to Paris for the weekend.' She stopped suddenly, biting her lip. 'Look, I shouldn't be saying all this. I don't know what you must be thinking. I'm not normally such a watering pot.' Her lips stretched into a quivering smile. 'It must be my hormones. But I'll stop embarrassing myself—and everyone else—and go back to Bristol.' She paused. 'You've been very kind. What's your name?'

Olivia prayed that the floor would open and swallow her.

She said, 'Olivia Butler, Mrs Attwood.' She looked down at the tiles at her feet, willing them apart.

There was a silence, then Maria said, 'Ah,' very quietly. She left the bathroom, closing the door behind her.

Olivia slumped against the wall, feeling sick to her stomach. Everything she'd ever said to Jeremy, every kiss, every caress was coming back to haunt her.

He lied, she thought exhaustedly. Whatever their problems were, Maria wanted to find a solution. That doesn't make her the hard-nosed bitch he claimed.

She made no attempt to sponge her dress.

I deserve to have champagne thrown over me—and worse, she thought miserably. I never thought of her as another human being—as someone who could cry and suffer. As someone who cared. I only wish she could know how deeply I'm suffering too.

It was as if a veil had been torn aside to reveal a gaping wound. Only who was the wounded one—Maria or herself?

Oh, Declan, she thought achingly. How could you tell her? How could you be so cruel?

She walked back into the bedroom, and came face to face with Jeremy.

He said hurriedly, 'I heard you'd arrived. I've been looking for you. Listen, Livvy, about these things Declan's been saying…'

'They don't matter,' she said quietly. 'Nothing matters except that I never want to see either of you again. Goodbye.'

She went out into the living room. It was still packed, but she could see Declan's tall figure by the window, with Melinda's red hair close by, as if she was pinned to him.

Across the noise of music, chatter and laughter she thought she heard him call her name, but she didn't stop.

And when she was out in the street, she began to run.

CHAPTER ELEVEN

OLIVIA was breathless and panting by the time she reached Lancey Terrace, stumbling in her high heels.

Hand pressed to her side, she stood for a moment, leaning against the wrought-iron gates leading into the garden, trying to calm herself. To get back in control.

In her head, she could still hear Declan's voice calling her name, and she'd run because she was frightened he'd come after her. And she couldn't face him now, she thought. Her sense of betrayal was too deep.

Their so-called truce was over for good. And smashed alongside it was every foolish hope, every impossible dream.

All she needed now was a corner to hide in. She straightened, opening her small black bag and fumbling in it for her keys. But the key that emerged first was the one to the garden, which she must have inadvertently picked up with the others.

She turned it in her hand, staring down at it in the lamplight, then turned, with sudden resolution, and fitted it into the lock.

After all, she reasoned, if someone was indeed looking for her, the flat would be the place to target. So she wouldn't go home at once. She'd walk, and try to get her breath back, and her head together.

It was a warm night, the air heavy and humid, but Olivia shivered as a stray breeze touched her bare shoulders and arms. In her headlong flight she'd forgotten all about her jacket, she realised with vexation. She wrapped her arms across her body, hugging herself as she walked.

It was dark now, and the lights were on in the houses.

Olivia glanced sideways into uncurtained windows as she passed, thinking how safe and cosy it all looked. And yet in every house the game of life went on, with sadness, betrayal, reconciliation and compromise. No one was immune.

She shivered again, but from a sense of isolation rather than chill.

Common sense dictated that at this time of night she should stick to the gravelled walk round the perimeter, but she turned off just the same, making her way across the centre of the garden, her steps unerring in spite of the darkness because she'd walked the same route so many times. Bound for her own private sanctuary.

She sat down, huddling herself into a corner of the bench as if she wished to make herself invisible, waiting for the peace of the place to touch her.

But the usual alchemy didn't seem to be working. Her head seemed to be filled with images—Maria Attwood's pain-filled eyes, Melinda's predatory, possessive fingers hooked into Declan's arm, Jeremy's evasive expression.

But it was Declan she saw most, the silvery eyes stormy and full of anger. But not filled with guilt—the acknowledgement of betrayal that she'd have expected. Or even any regret for the hurt he'd caused.

How could he? she thought, her throat tightening convulsively. Oh, how could he? And the first scalding tear trickled down her cold face.

She wept silently, her head bowed, her body rigid. Around her, she could hear all the noises of the night—the rustle of the wind in the leaves, the yowl of a marauding cat, a swift burst of music as someone opened then closed a window, and in the distance a faint rumble of thunder. The fluttering breeze brought the scent of rain.

She thought, It's time I was getting back. She lifted her hands, scrubbing her eyes as a child might do, then stood up.

The bushes parted and stirred, and a narrow beam of light

caught her, held her. As she shaded her eyes from the dazzle Declan said grimly, 'I guessed I'd find you here.'

'Go away from me.' Her voice shook. 'Leave me alone.'

'Don't be a little fool. We have to talk.'

'There's nothing to talk about. You've already said everything—and to Maria. You told her I was having an affair with Jeremy—even though you knew—you must have known...' Her voice broke. 'Oh, what's the use?'

'Listen to me, and listen well.' His voice was soft but resonant. 'I told Maria nothing of the kind. She's still in total ignorance about your ill-conceived passion for her worthless husband, and that's the way it's going to stay.'

'But she knew who I was,' she protested. 'She knew my name.'

'Then she heard it in another context.' There was a further growl of thunder, closer this time, and the first swirl of heavy raindrops. 'But we can't stand here discussing the matter. We'll be drenched. Come on in the house.' The flashlight played over her. 'Mother of God, where's your jacket?'

'I left it behind,' she said furiously. 'And I'm going nowhere with you.'

'Well, you're not staying here to catch pneumonia.' The light clicked off, and two swift strides brought him to her side. Before she could register what was happening, he'd lifted her bodily, hoisting her over his shoulder.

For a moment she was stunned—rendered dumb with outrage. Then she began to pound his back with her fists. 'Put me down. Put me down at once.'

'It'll be a pleasure,' he said. 'Once we're indoors out of this rain. And stop wriggling, damn you.' And he administered an admonitory tap to her rear.

She would have yelled, but being carried at speed through heavy rain with her head dangling towards the ground wasn't conducive to anything but a few grunts of discomfort, she discovered.

But once they were inside the French windows, and he'd lowered her to the floor, she found her voice easily enough.

'You bastard.' She was shaking with rage—and another, very different emotion that she didn't wish to examine too closely. 'Do you realise how many assault charges I can bring against you?'

Declan finished securing the French windows and looked at her.

He said slowly, 'Then I may as well be hanged for a sheep as lamb.' And he walked across to her and took her in his arms.

He wasn't gentle. His kiss was fuelled by anger. And the same emotion sparked her response. Their mouths explored hungrily, made predatory by the same burning need. She felt the heat of his tongue against hers. And instead of trying to push him away her hands curled into the folds of his shirt, holding him closer.

When they broke apart they were gasping, their gazes locked, like opponents measuring each other. Or as if a spell had been cast, binding them together throughout eternity.

The lights flickered suddenly, and the thunder roared almost overhead, making Olivia jump.

'Heavens.' Her laugh shook with nervousness, and she shivered.

Declan drew a breath, his hand closing on her bare shoulder. 'You're freezing. Come with me.'

She found herself going with him up the stairs and into a large square room, with another set of French windows opening on to a wrought-iron balcony beyond. The walls and carpet were the colour of warm sand, and two big sofas covered in deep green linen flanked an elaborate marble fireplace. One wall, she saw, was composed solely of bookshelves.

Declan had gone through a concealed door at the back of the room, but he was back almost at once, carrying a navy silk robe that she recognised.

'Go and have a shower while I organise a hot drink,' he directed crisply. 'Your dress needs drying, so leave it out.'

She said huskily, 'Lend me an umbrella and I'll go home.'

He turned at the door, his brows lifting. He said quietly, 'Ah, no, Olivia. We both know better than that.'

The hot water stung her skin, reviving her magically. She reduced the temperature and let it flow through her hair, as if she was performing some ritual cleansing, ridding herself of the evening's dirt and wretchedness.

She towelled herself until her skin glowed. She combed her damp hair back from her face, staring at herself critically in the mirror. She looked pale, but her lips were reddened and slightly swollen, and she touched them gently with the tip of her finger. Remembering.

Declan's robe was far too big, so she wrapped it round her, then wound the sash round her slim waist, anchoring it securely. The sleeves were too long, too, and she turned them back almost to her elbows.

She thought, I look like a geisha...

A faint scent of the cologne he used still clung to the robe. Eyes closed, she breathed it, then lifted a fold of the silk to her cheek and held it there.

When she went back into the drawing room Declan was seated on one of the sofas, a tray of coffee on the table in front of him, pouring cognac into goblets.

He said, 'You'll be glad to know the storm's passed over.' He studied her, a smile touching his eyes. 'And the robe looks better on you.'

A mixture of shyness and excitement tangled in her throat. 'I don't think so.' She stood behind the sofa opposite, resting her hands on its padded back. She said, 'I shouldn't be here.'

'Give me one good reason.' His voice was calm.

'Your cousin...'

'Maria's gone to an old schoolfriend in Chelsea. She needs a woman to talk to tonight. Ellie's a great girl. She'll hold her and comfort her, and pour drink into her, then put her on the train back when she's ready. Now come and have your coffee.'

She didn't move. She said, 'Jeremy never gave a damn about me, did he? Not from the first. I suppose I was just a novelty because I wouldn't go to bed with him. Maria said there's always been other women.'

'Yes.' His voice was gentle.

'He made me believe he cared for me while we were in Bristol, but when I came here everything changed. But I didn't want to admit it.' She paused. 'The weekend of my birthday—he said there was a conference, but I knew somehow that there wasn't.'

Declan nodded, his face carefully expressionless. 'He was at a hotel in the New Forest—with Melinda.'

'Melinda,' she echoed shakily. 'But she's your girlfriend.'

'No,' he said, swiftly and sharply. 'We had a brief affair, but that was over a long time ago. Since then she's been engaged to a mate of mine. But some friends of his were also enjoying the New Forest, and saw Melinda, so the engagement's off.'

'But she was with you tonight.' She'd given herself away with that small painful protest, she realised with dismay.

'No,' Declan said forcefully. 'We were in the same room, so she attached herself for a while, that's all. She's an actress, with ambitions to get into TV as a presenter, and she's always seen me as a stepping stone in her career plan.'

He looked at Olivia gravely. 'She met Jeremy here, of course, then they ran into each other at some promotional thing.'

His mouth twisted. 'I gather he exaggerated his earnings, prospects and general importance to impress her, and it worked.' He shook his head. 'But I think he was a little shaken to discover how expensive her favours can be. Bill Fenner's actually had a lucky escape.'

She said slowly, 'Jeremy said the weekend had been dire.'

'I'm sure his credit cards thought so,' Declan said drily. 'But she must have persuaded him that she was worth it, because they were here together while I was in Ireland. I came back earlier than I intended and caught them. And threw him out as a consequence.'

He sighed sharply. 'Then Maria turned up out of the blue, wanting to see him, expecting him to be around. So I had to tell her where he was—and why.'

'How could you?'

He said simply. 'Because she asked me. And though I've tried to protect her up to now, by keeping things from her, I've never lied to her.'

'Couldn't you have stopped her going to the party?'

'I tried,' he said drily. 'But she's a hard woman to convince. And she had a good reason for confronting him.'

Olivia looked at him gravely. 'She's going to have a baby—isn't she?'

His mouth tightened, and he nodded.

'But surely, now he knows that, he'll come to his senses. He'll make an effort.'

'She hasn't told him. She went to the party, checked the situation for herself, and decided to call it a day.'

'But she still cares about him. And how will she manage with the baby?'

'No one said it would be easy. But she's a tough girl, and her mind's made up. He's had all the last chances he's going to get.'

He gave her a straight look. 'Jeremy's never wanted children. He married Maria for her earning potential. When they lived in Bristol he was always getting into debt, and expecting her to bail him out. When she wanted to move to London with him, he wouldn't let her. Told her she was doing too well at work, and she ought to wait until she got an equally good offer up here.'

'He lied about everything, didn't he?'

'Pretty much. I'm sorry, Olivia.'

'Don't say that,' she said quietly. 'I was a blind idiot. It's Maria who deserves the sympathy.'

He shrugged, his face bleak. 'She wanted a life. He wanted a lifestyle. End of story. Now come and drink this coffee while it's still hot.'

She sat down, facing him, arranging the skirt of the robe decorously. She cupped the bowl of the brandy goblet in her hand, breathing the cognac's powerful aroma.

She said, 'Is Melinda moving into the flat with him?'

'God knows, but I almost hope so. There's a pair that deserve each other.'

Which surprised a laugh out of her. 'Yes—yes, they do.'

He'd lit the gas fire in the grate, and she watched the leap of the flames as she drank her coffee and sipped the cognac appreciatively.

There was a silence between them, but not the taut, aloof silence of recent days. This was a quietude—tranquil—almost companionable. She smiled to herself at the thought, and looked at him, and saw his eyes on her, and realised, with a catch of breath, that she was wrong.

She hurried into speech. 'Do you think my dress is dry by now?'

'I'll check it presently.'

'Only I really should be going. It's late…'

'And tomorrow's Sunday. There's nothing to rush for. Or are you really so desperate to get away from me?'

'It's not that.' She looked down at her clasped hands. 'But I don't know why you brought me here.'

'Ah, yes.' There was a ghost of laughter in his voice. 'You do.'

She shook her head, aware that her breathing was flurried. 'I just don't understand—anything.'

He said quietly, 'Did I scare you earlier—downstairs?'

'No.'

'Because I frightened myself,' he went on meditatively. 'I went to Ireland to get away from you, but you came with me every step of the way. You rode with me, walked with me, and smiled through my dreams. So when I saw you standing in front of me, touching you became a total necessity. And I forgot to be gentle.'

Olivia raised her head and met his eyes. Saw the tension in him. The unaccustomed diffidence. The question in his gaze that she alone could answer.

And realised nothing else mattered but giving him the response he needed.

She said softly, 'I'm not glass, Declan. I won't break.'

'Show me.' His voice was husky.

She rose, and walked round the table to stand in front of him. She untied the sash and let the robe fall open. Declan made a small sound in his throat as he looked at her. Then his hands slid round her, under the folds of silk, pulling her closer until he buried his face in the rounded softness of her body, his mouth burning against her skin.

She cradled his head in her hands, bending to press her own lips to his dark hair in silent offering. In acceptance.

He drew her slowly down to him, until she was lying in his arms across his body, looking up at him with eyes made drowsy by desire.

He began to kiss her, his mouth brushing hers lightly and wickedly, coaxing her lips to part for him. His hand stroked the curve of her shoulder, pushing the robe away, then travelled down to cup her breast. His fingers teased her nipple, enticing it to stand erect, eager for the soft caress of his tongue.

As his mouth moved downwards to possess its roundness her body arched in sweet voluptuous enjoyment.

His hand explored her, moving slowly down her body, tracing small erotic patterns on her skin. Every pulse, every nerve-ending was coming to singing life beneath his touch.

His mouth moved back to hers, kissing her deeply, achingly, while his hand moulded the slender curve of her hip, then slid down to her parted thighs, enjoying the moist silken heat of her with sensuous mastery.

Her faint moan of pleasure trembled under his lips as his caress slowed, deepened, focusing on the tiny centre of her delight. She surrendered herself completely to the exquisite torment, aware that her self-control was fracturing, but uncaring. Knowing only that she was being carried inexorably, but with total trust, to some edge.

And when the moment came—when the world splintered into spasm after spasm of undreamed of rapture—his arms held her strongly and safely, and his heartbeat echoed against hers.

When it was over, she lay quietly, mindless and weightless, letting her fevered breathing slow, her lips pressed to the pulse in his throat. And felt herself lifted gently, carried out of the lamplit room into the shadows where his bed waited for them.

She lay, watching through half-closed eyes as Declan stripped off his clothes, her mouth curving sensuously in appreciation and anticipation.

When he came to lie beside her naked her arms welcomed him, her body shivering with pleasure as the warmth of his skin touched hers.

He kissed her without haste, savouring her mouth, the delicacy of her cheekbones, and the lids of her wondering eyes.

'Touch me,' he whispered, as his lips found the curve of her ear and the graceful line of her throat.

She obeyed, shyly at first, running her hands across the muscular shoulders and over the powerful contours of his back. She wasn't a virgin, but she wasn't experienced either, and she felt strangely at a loss.

'What's wrong?' He'd sensed her hesitation.

'I wish I knew more—about pleasing men.'

He was shaken with sudden laughter, his hand tenderly stroking the hair back from her damp forehead. 'How many are you planning on?'

She grazed his shoulder with her teeth. 'You know what I mean.'

'Yes.' His voice was very gentle. 'But I want you just the way you are, Olivia. Nothing we've learned from others can ever apply to our experience of each other. And what we need to know we can learn together.'

His mouth drifted softly down her body, discovering every pulse-point, each sensitive, responsive inch of skin. She moved against him, murmuring her pleasure, her caressing hands gaining confidence as she sought the velvet strength of him, making him groan softly in turn.

She longed to yield completely—to feel him inside her—all-male, all-powerful.

'I want you.' She breathed the words.

'Take me,' he whispered huskily, the silvery eyes slumbrous and intent. 'I'm yours.'

Slowly, she guided him to her—teased him deliciously for a moment, then lifted herself against him, sheathing him in passionate completion.

'Ah, my love.' The words seemed torn from his throat. 'My love.'

He moved slowly at first, as if relishing each long, lingering thrust, and she followed, the motion of her body matching his sweetly, almost languidly.

Then, as she felt the first quiver of ultimate response, her arms held him more fiercely. Her slender legs embraced his hips in wordless urging.

Their mouths came together greedily, demandingly as his possession of her deepened—quickened—carrying them both with utter certainty towards the agonised bliss of climax.

There was a moment when she thought she was dying—that her body would not survive this feverish ravishment. She cried out, and heard his voice answer as if the sound had been wrenched from him.

Then the world steadied, and she felt the reality of his sweat-slicked shoulders under her hands as she floated back to earth.

* * *

A long time later, Declan said, 'I thought at one time I'd have to build a willow cabin.'

'A what?' She turned her head and stared at him, then remembered. 'Oh—*Twelfth Night.*'

'''And make the babbling gossip of the air Cry out, 'Olivia!''' he quoted softly. '''O! you should not rest Between the elements of air and earth, But you should pity me!'''

She stretched bonelessly, like a kitten. 'Is that all it was—sympathy?'

He laughed, and drew her closer. 'I can think of no other reason.'

Her hand smoothed his hair-roughened chest. 'That's the kind of modesty that's almost immodest.'

'Then I'd better change tack.' He dropped a light kiss on her mouth. 'Have some more champagne.'

'Mmm.' Olivia sighed luxuriously as he refilled her glass. 'This is incredibly decadent.'

'Well, make the most of it, woman,' he said with mock severity. 'Next time it's a cup of strong tea and a bacon sandwich. I need to keep my strength up.'

She grinned impishly at him. 'Sounds good to me. I'm starving.'

'Ah, God, my perfect girl.' He kissed her again, spilling her champagne down her body.

'Oh, look what you've done,' she scolded. 'I'm soaked.'

'What a waste entirely,' he murmured. He sighed, lowering his mouth to her breasts. 'I'll just have to salvage what I can...'

The bacon sandwiches were wonderful, and Olivia demolished every scrap.

'You're a great chef.'

'Hmm.' Declan frowned critically. 'The bacon could have been crisper. I need more practice.' He smiled at her across the table. 'Like every night for the rest of our lives.'

She felt the colour rise in her face as she smiled back at him, her heart lifting.

She thought—This, I shall remember always. This moment of complete happiness. For the times that aren't so golden.

And stopped, as a faint shiver of disquiet stirred deep within her. As if, she thought, some shadow had indeed fallen across her joy.

But that, she told herself, was nonsense. Because she and Declan belonged to each other now. And nothing could spoil that. Nothing.

CHAPTER TWELVE

WHEN she awoke, the room was full of watery sunlight, and she was occupying the big bed alone.

She propped herself up on her elbow, wondering where Declan had gone and taking her first good look at the room in which she'd spent the most heavenly night of her life.

It was large and airy, with a big window framed in long cream drapes. The walls were a pale terracotta, and the wooden floor was covered in Mexican rugs in primitive earth colours. Apart from the bed, with its cream covers, the room contained little furniture. There was a television and video unit on a stand, a pair of night-tables in some dark wood, and an antique chest of drawers.

It was a very calm, uncluttered room, she decided, rather like the rest of the house.

And very much as she herself felt on this fine Sunday morning, she thought, with a small private smile. But wasn't terrific sex supposed to iron out the creases and make you see with a new clarity?

I never knew, she thought shaking her head. I never realised how it could be.

None of her previous limited experience had prepared her for the totality of her response to Declan's lovemaking. For her unexpected capacity to give and receive delight.

And she had delighted him. He had told her so in a hundred different ways—and not just in words.

She ached pleasurably in all kinds of places, she realised as she stretched languidly. But that was to be expected, considering they'd eventually fallen asleep in each other's arms in complete exhaustion.

She heard a rustle of paper, and, turning her head

sharply, saw that her outflung hand had encountered a note pinned to the adjoining pillow.

She unfolded it and scanned the brief message: 'Gone to buy us some breakfast. Stay where you are for room service.'

She was tempted, she thought as she pushed back the covers, her mouth curving reminiscently. But the least she could do was put the coffee on.

She showered swiftly, slipping into her underwear and shoes, which she'd left in the bathroom. Until she could find her dress, it would have to be Declan's robe again, she decided, fastening the sash as she went downstairs.

She'd just reached the hall when the front door opened behind her. She spun round, smiling mischievously, intending to tell him he'd returned five minutes too soon. And then the words and the smile died on her lips as she found herself facing Jeremy.

For a moment there was total silence. Olivia stood as if rooted to the spot, her lips parted in shock. Jeremy looked her over, eyes narrowed, his mouth twisting unpleasantly.

'Well, well,' he said softly. 'Who'd have thought it?'

She found her own voice. 'What are you doing here? And how did you get in?'

'The door was on the latch. And I could ask what you're doing, too, but I don't have to, because it's bloody obvious what's been going on.' He gave a sneering laugh. 'You were too pure and righteous to let me put a hand on you, and now you're sleeping with the boss. Tut, tut, Livvy. What a little hypocrite you are.'

The robe covered her from her throat to her feet, but she felt naked suddenly. And ridiculously scared.

She lifted her chin defiantly. 'It has nothing to do with you...'

'Now that's where you're wrong. It has everything to do with me, as I've just realised.' He began to laugh. 'My God, I knew Declan would do a lot for his beloved cousin Maria, but I never dreamed he'd go to these lengths. Yet I should have known, because he told me what he intended to do—right here in this hall. Only I was too dumb to see it—then.'

'What are you talking about?'

'Bait, sweetie,' Jeremy said contemptuously. 'Declan decided he was going to split us up by leading you astray. Giving you a taste of his famous sexual prowess. Except that he served up the full banquet by the look of you. So, he offered himself as bait, and you couldn't wait to wriggle on to his hook—could you, darling? He even moved you into his office to make sure of you.'

He laughed again. 'Poor, naive little Livvy. All the bastard had to do was reel you in. And now he'll throw you back with the other little fishes.'

She drew a deep, painful breath. 'I don't believe you.'

Only she did believe it. She'd even thought of it herself, she remembered frantically. Considered it as a possibility. Then discounted it. And now it was back to haunt her as grim reality.

'You forget. I've lived with him.' His tone was vindictive. 'I've seen how he operates—and I'm a mere beginner by comparison. Let's see—he romanced you into bed last night, and now he's out buying the usual croissants and Buck's Fizz for your farewell feast. All quite routine, I assure you.'

'You've lied to me for months—and you're lying now.'

He shrugged. 'I've no reason. Actually, I feel sorry for you, allowing yourself to be taken in like this. Face it, love, if he wasn't so devoted to my bitch of a wife and her interests, he wouldn't have given you a second look. Declan dates models, actresses, girls who're at the top of their particular tree—like that blonde designer he was seeing.'

He shook his head. 'You fell for the dangerous charm, darling, and failed to see the barracuda underneath. But then the devious bastard's been making fools of us both.'

'Stop it.' Olivia tried to cover her ears with her hands.

'Oh, dear,' Jeremy mocked. 'Getting through to you, is

it, that you haven't been the world's cleverest bunny? But cheer up. You've been laid by an expert, and that kind of education is never wasted. The next guy along will be incredibly grateful.'

'You disgust me.'

'Now that's not very kind.' He couldn't control his malicious glee. 'He's the one who's conned you—used you.'

She looked at him steadily. 'And you didn't?'

'Guilty as charged,' he said nonchalantly. 'But you have to admit you were the perfect decoy—the old childhood friend—needy and a little sad—who wanted a brotherly shoulder to cry on. Even the most suspicious wife wouldn't have worried about that. You were the perfect alibi.

'Oh, I'm not saying I wouldn't have had you if you'd been available,' he added with another shrug. 'And the rent would have been useful. But you were fixated on love and marriage, and that's not my scene.

'And it's not Declan's either—in case you were stupid enough to hope.'

She said, 'Get out.'

'Willingly. I only came round to do you a favour.' He held up a plastic carrier. 'Your jacket. Melinda doesn't want it cluttering up the flat. I couldn't get an answer at your place, so it occurred to me that Declan could return it to you at work tomorrow. But this is better still.'

He tossed the carrier to her, and she caught it, hugging it against her breasts as if it were a shield.

'So tell me about him, Livvy.' His voice was low suddenly. Suggestive. 'Give me a few tips. Make me eat my heart out. What does he do in bed that keeps his women hanging round panting for more?'

She felt as if she'd been covered in slime. She stared back at him, sickened, unable to speak.

'Although I wouldn't bother in your case, darling,' he went on. 'I doubt if you've made his A list. Because he has one, and he gives his women scores out of ten. Maria told me that ages ago. It's the only time I ever heard her disapprove of him. Think about it.'

He blew her a kiss, and went.

Olivia stood for a long moment, staring into space. She felt numb, but that wouldn't last. Soon—too soon—there would be unbearable pain. And a sense of humiliation going too deep for words.

She thought, I have to get out of here. Now. Before he comes back.

Her bag was in the dining room, and she found her dress draped over a clothes airer in the small laundry room that opened off the kitchen.

She took off the robe and threw it down, feeling her skin burn where it had touched. But at least she could change down here, she thought as she zipped up her dress. She didn't have to die the death of going back to Declan's bedroom—the scene of her bitter, unforgivable betrayal.

She heard herself moan softly, and dragged her jacket out of the bag, shaking out the creases.

'Olivia?' She'd been so intent on making her escape that she hadn't heard his return, but he was standing in the doorway watching her, his brows lifted questioningly. 'You're dressed. What happened to breakfast in bed?'

'I changed my mind.' How could her voice sound so normal? 'I don't really care for croissants and Buck's Fizz.'

'Fair enough,' he said equably. 'Because I've brought a stack of bacon—in case we need more midnight snacks—plus eggs, tomatoes, and sausages. The full Irish breakfast. Oh, and a couple of baguettes with some pâté and fruit for lunch.'

'I won't be staying. Not for breakfast, lunch, or even another minute.' She shrugged on her jacket.

'What the hell is this?' He was frowning now. 'And where did that come from?' He pointed at the jacket.

'Jeremy brought it round. Wasn't that kind of him? You left the door on the latch and he just walked in.'

'Oh, God, I'm sorry.' He sounded genuinely remorseful,

she thought with incredulity. 'It never occurred to me he'd have the brass face to turn up here. But surely he can't have upset you again?'

'On the contrary.' Inside the pockets of her jacket, her hands were balled into fists. 'He's done me a number of favours. Now, if you'll excuse me, I'll be going.'

'Not like this.' Declan stepped forward, taking her by the shoulders. 'I won't let you.'

'Don't touch me.' Olivia recoiled, shaking herself free almost violently. 'You'll never lay a hand on me again.'

For a moment he stared at her in total disbelief, then he took a careful pace backwards, raising his hands in the air.

'You're free.' His drawl held menace. 'But I think I merit an explanation.'

She walked past him, careful to avoid even the slightest contact. She couldn't afford to remember even fleetingly how his body had felt against hers—inside hers. Last night he'd turned her into his creature—wild, uninhibited, sobbing with ecstasy in his arms. This morning she belonged to herself again.

He followed her to the dining room. Watched while she retrieved her bag.

He said, 'I'm waiting, Olivia.'

She faced him, chin lifted. 'Your devotion to your cousin is admirable, Declan, but I didn't realise the lengths your protectiveness could take you. I now know that you set out to seduce me simply to separate me from Jeremy.'

'What are you talking about?' She saw the colour fade from his face.

'Are you denying you used yourself as bait—taking me to dinner—the job—my birthday treat?' She spat the words at him, using her anger to dam back the hurt tears that were perilously close but which she could not afford to shed.

And at the same time part of her was praying that he would indeed deny it. Condemn Jeremy as a liar. Banish her own terrifying doubts for ever.

But all she saw in his face was shock—and guilt.

She said, 'Can you deny it? You said you never lied to Maria, so do me the same courtesy.'

He took a deep breath. 'No, but you have to let me explain...'

'No explanation's necessary. That's all I wanted to know.' She walked to the French windows. 'Although I can't understand why you went on with the plan even when you knew I'd finished with Jeremy. Perhaps you couldn't resist another notch on your overcrowded bedpost. Or maybe it was a reward because I'd been a good girl—not made waves for Maria. Was that it?'

He said, in a voice she barely recognised, 'I thought it was love.'

'Love?' Olivia echoed derisively. 'You don't even know the meaning of the word. You see, I've heard about your A list, too, and I'm compiling one of my own. A list of people with decency, integrity and common humanity. And do you know something, Declan? You won't even feature.'

She opened the French windows and walked out into the sunlight without looking back.

Out of his life, she thought. Back into her own. And an eternity of loneliness and despair.

Olivia switched off the word processor and sat back with a faint sigh. Another week over, she thought. Another weekend to face.

Work had been her lifesaver. Her last line of defence. And her present job, replacing a secretary on sick leave in a busy chambers in Gray's Inn, left her, thankfully, with no time to think. Maybe she should look for something to occupy her during the endless weekends, too, she mused. A job in a wine bar, perhaps, or showing property.

Sandra Wilton had been knocked sideways when Olivia had presented herself at the agency with the announcement that she was not returning to Academy Productions, but

she'd seen the other girl's white face and burning eyes, and
had tactfully refrained from asking too many questions.

And any fears Olivia had had about being blacklisted by
the agency or treated as unreliable had soon been assuaged.

The move to Wandsworth had been a relief too. She'd
told herself that Declan wouldn't come after her to Lancey
Terrace, and she'd been right, but she still hadn't felt safe
there. It had been altogether too close for comfort, and she
couldn't risk the pain of running into him on the street, or
even seeing him from a distance.

'Goodnight, Olivia.' Tim Carney, one of the pupils in
the chambers, stopped beside her desk. 'Have a good weekend.'

'Thank you.' She glanced up, forcing a smile. 'You too.'

He lingered. 'Actually, a few of us are going for a drink.
We wondered whether you'd like to join us.'

'That's very kind, but I'm afraid I can't.' He was good-
looking, talented and pleasant, she thought dispassionately.
And anyone in her right mind wouldn't hesitate. Only she
wasn't in her right mind. She inhabited a kind of bleak
chaos, where nothing made sense any more.

He bit his lip. 'Ah, well. Another time, perhaps.'

'Perhaps,' she agreed gently.

Autumn had come swiftly and sharply, with early frosts,
and as she walked to the bus stop dried leaves were swirling
down from the trees and crunching under her feet. The grey
skies and chill in the air suited her mood perfectly, only
now she had to go home to Wandsworth and pretend everything was fine.

Her room was small, but she had it to herself and the
walls were solid, so only she knew that she cried herself
to sleep each night. And only she knew how her body still
yearned for Declan, no matter how her mind might reject
him. That was something she simply had to endure.

When she'd moved into the flat, she'd feared that Louise
might chatter on endlessly about Academy Productions, but
apart from mentioning that Carol had left with equal sud-

denness—'It must be catching, Livvy'—and that Declan
was striding about these days like Son of Terminator and
no one could get near him, she'd said nothing.

Of course, Declan's weekly political television programme had returned—'Tougher than ever' said the crit-
ics—but Olivia contrived to be out of the sitting room while
it was being shown.

Her only weakness had been to keep the paperweight
he'd given her, hidden at the bottom of a drawer. She'd put
it outside with the rubbish, then retrieved it at the last minute, unable to let it go.

One day, she told herself, she'd be strong enough to get
rid of it permanently. And then, maybe, she'd know she
was healed.

A big advantage of flat-sharing was that you didn't have
to cook every night, she thought, her nose twitching appreciatively as she let herself in. Tonight it was the turn of
Hilary, the Casserole Queen, and there was a tantalisingly
savoury aroma in the air.

'Listen,' Louise said, appearing in the doorway of
Olivia's room. 'We're going to this new club that Hilary
knows of later on. Are you up to it?'

'Not really, thanks.' Olivia flexed her shoulders. 'I've
had a really busy day, so I'm planning on an early night.'

Louise sighed. 'We'll prise you out one evening, see if
we don't. But if you really won't come, can I borrow your
little black bag? The catch has gone on mine.'

'Yes, it's hanging on the back of the door. Help yourself.' Olivia kicked off her shoes.

'You've left something inside,' Louise said, delving. She
produced a large iron key. 'What's this?'

'Oh, heavens,' Olivia said slowly. 'It's the key to Lancey
Gardens. I must have forgotten to hand it back with the
others. I—I haven't used that bag since I came here.'

'Well, no harm done,' Louise said cheerfully. 'You'll
have to drop it off some time, that's all.' And she
whizzed off.

Olivia looked down at the key. Yes, she thought. I suppose I will.

Her stomach was churning as she walked along Lancey Terrace the following afternoon. She was sorely tempted to turn back, and post the key to Sasha. But as she telephoned to make sure her ex-landlady would be at home that would be neither kind nor fair. Particularly as Sasha had sounded so thrilled to hear from her.

'Darling child.' Sasha enveloped her in a scented embrace. She stood back, giving Olivia a critical look. 'You've lost weight, and you can't afford to. And so pale, too. Come in. I've just made a pot of coffee.'

Humph warbled at her, then circled her three times, and jumped on to her lap as soon as she sat down.

'You see, we all miss you.' Sasha poured the coffee.

'I'm really sorry about taking the key.' Olivia produced it.

'Don't worry about it. The boy who took your flat doesn't want it. The garden's not his thing, as it was yours.'

'No,' Olivia said with constraint. She put the key down on the table in front of her.

'Darling,' Sasha said gently. 'Is there anything you'd like to talk about? I can't bear to see you look so sad.'

'There's nothing,' Olivia said. 'Except that I'm probably going back to Bristol.' She forced a smile. 'I don't think London suits me.'

Sasha sighed. 'Well, don't decide anything too hastily. Perhaps you and London haven't given each other a proper chance.' She paused. 'Is there anything you want to ask me—about anyone?'

The muscles tightened in Olivia's throat. 'No.'

'He looks so dreadful,' Sasha went on, as if Olivia hadn't spoken. 'He doesn't smile. He's like a stranger. And I feel almost sorry for some of those poor people he interviews. Everyone's saying he goes too far these days.'

Olivia stared down at her coffee. She said with difficulty,

'Do you remember the sundial in the garden? The inscription says, "Time makes Love pass." Do you think it's true?'

'Oh, my dear girl, of course not,' Sasha told her sadly. 'When love is real and true it lasts for ever.' Her eyes were misty. 'When I think of my beloved it's as if we'd just met. As if he's waiting for me at some turn in the path. That's how it must be.'

She pushed the key back towards Olivia. 'Keep it for a while, darling. Come back sometimes, and walk in the garden. Humph will go with you if you want company. And he doesn't mind if you cry, either. He's been such a comfort to me. Sit, and feel the sun on your face before the winter comes. It's such a healing place. It helped me so much when I lost my beloved. And it will help you. I know it.'

But your memories are happy ones, Olivia thought wistfully as she reluctantly replaced the key in her bag. I can't cure my pain unless I wipe out the past completely. And that's not possible.

There was a smell of smoke in the air as she paused at the gates, and a thin blue trail rising in the air where someone was burning leaves.

There was a raw feeling in the air, and a lot of the shrubs and trees had bare branches already, Olivia noticed, turning up her coat collar. But the clearing with the sundial was surrounded by evergreens, so it still retained the sense of being cut off from the rest of the world.

The bench felt slightly damp, so she decided not to sit down. Instead, she walked over to the sundial, and ran her fingers over the inscription.

She would just have to pray that Sasha was wrong, she thought with a pang, and turned, sighing, to go.

Declan was standing a few yards away, just inside the clearing. He was wearing jeans, and a dark blue sweater with a roll collar. He looked haggard, and as if he hadn't slept for weeks.

He said hoarsely, 'Olivia. You're here.'

She said bitterly, 'I suppose Sasha tipped you off?'

'No.' Declan shook his head. 'I've been here every day. Waiting for you. I told myself if I was patient you'd come eventually.'

Her heart twisted inside her. She said crisply, 'And now I'm going.'

He took a step towards her. 'Not yet. Not until I've had a chance to talk to you—to explain…'

'I had all the explanation I needed—that morning—when you couldn't look me in the face.' Pain clutched her again at the memory.

'What do you want me to say?' There was anguish in his voice. 'That the thought of taking you away from that cheating bastard never occurred to me? I can't. And I did taunt him with it. He was right about that, damn him. And I'm not proud of it. In some ways I deserved every harsh word you flung at me when you walked out on me.' His voice deepened passionately. 'But everything changed after we had dinner together. You must have known that.'

She said wearily, 'I don't think I know anything any more.'

'And do you think I wasn't confused too? To have all my assumptions about you suddenly challenged like that?' He bit his lip. 'I wanted to believe you were as worthless as Jeremy himself. I—needed to think that, because I didn't want to face the fact that I was fighting something inside myself.'

'Oh, really?' She lifted her chin scornfully. 'Next you'll be telling me it was really love at first sight.'

'No,' he said. 'Although you were there, in my head, from that first moment. But I told myself that was anger—because you were going to hurt Maria. Only it wasn't that simple.'

He paused. 'When I kissed you that night, I was knocked out by your reaction. I could feel you trembling in my arms, taste the innocence on your lips. Believe me, Olivia, the hardest thing I ever did in my life was walk away and leave you.'

He looked at her pleadingly. 'Don't you see? If I'd been the villain you think, I'd have stayed. Coaxed you into inviting me into your flat. Persuaded you to let me spend the night. Because I could have done. Isn't that the truth?'

In spite of herself, she felt her lips frame a silent, 'Yes.'

'Ah, my love,' he said softly. 'You were changing too.'

'But that doesn't change a thing.' She leant back against the sundial, the edge of the stone biting into her hands. 'You used me—manipulated me. Nothing can alter that.'

'Maybe not. But can't we learn from our mistakes—and be forgiven for them? Because that's what I'm asking you.' He threw his head back. 'Don't leave me, Olivia. I'll beg on my knees if you want.'

'Don't,' she said. 'It's over, Declan. You fooled me once. But you don't have to pretend any more.'

'You think what we had together was pretence?' He closed his eyes wearily. 'Dear God, no one's that good an actor.' He looked at her, his eyes intense. 'Tell me you don't love me, Olivia. Swear it, and I'll let you go. But it had better be the truth, because if you leave me I'm only going to be half alive.'

'You mustn't say these things.' Her voice broke. 'It's cruel—and unfair.'

'No,' he said harshly. 'It's right—and it's real. I'm fighting for you, Olivia, and for our happiness. For our life together. Our unborn children. You're my woman, and nothing less will do.'

He looked at her pleadingly. 'Darling, my perfect girl, you must love me. You couldn't have made love with me as you did without loving me. That isn't the way you are. You're mine, and I'm yours, and there can't be any other way. I hurt you, and nothing can alter that, but I was hurting too, thinking it was still Jeremy you wanted.'

Olivia said nothing. She could recognize the pain in his

eyes, the loneliness and the fear. Recognise them because she shared them.

Only she didn't have to. And nor did he. Not any more. Never again. Because there could be forgiveness, and a new beginning. And, she realised shakily, all the happiness she could ever want in this world.

And somewhere deep inside her, in the cold, unhappy recesses of her soul, a tiny tendril of warmth and faith and trust was stirring into life. Defying the autumn chill. Coming into full, glorious bloom.

He threw his head back. 'I said everything changed when we had dinner together. What I didn't realise at first was how deep—how fundamental—the change had been. I didn't know I'd started to love you. Not then. Not immediately.

'Because I didn't expect that. If I'm honest, I didn't want it. I had my own plans.

'I went back to Ireland to sort my head out. To tell myself that you were still in love with Jeremy and I didn't have a prayer.'

His mouth twisted. 'But I couldn't stop talking about you, and at last my mother asked when she was going to meet her future daughter-in-law.

'And I knew then that, for better or worse, I had to come back. To make you see that Jeremy was no good, and that you belonged to me. To convince you, somehow, that I loved you, and wanted you as my wife. Because that was the truth and the whole truth.'

He sighed. 'I was on my way round to see you when Maria turned up. She needed my help, and I had to give it.'

'How—how is she?' Olivia asked.

'Hurting badly,' he said grimly. 'But her family have rallied round her, and she's staying with her parents. I gather she's already served divorce papers on Jeremy.'

He was silent for a moment. 'I didn't mean to make love to you that night. I came after you to comfort you—because

I was sure you'd be hurting too. I told myself I had to make you feel safe again—to win your trust. And instead I found myself in paradise.

'Now I've nothing, Olivia. Because when you went you took it all. Every hope—every dream. Come back, my darling. My one and only love. Make me human again.'

She was very still, her heart hammering with joy. With longing. With the promise of fulfilment and a love that would last for ever.

She said softly, a smile quivering on her lips, '''O! you should not rest Between the elements of air and earth, But you should pity me!'''

'Just pity?' It was a shadow of his old smile. And his eyes asked for reassurance, and absolution.

'No,' she said, her eyes radiant, her voice tender. 'Love.'

And she ran across the damp grass and into the sanctuary of Declan's waiting arms.

If you enjoyed what you just read,
then we've got an offer you can't resist!

Take 2 bestselling
love stories FREE!
Plus get a FREE surprise gift!

Clip this page and mail it to Harlequin Reader Service®

IN U.S.A.
3010 Walden Ave.
P.O. Box 1867
Buffalo, N.Y. 14240-1867

IN CANADA
P.O. Box 609
Fort Erie, Ontario
L2A 5X3

YES! Please send me 2 free Harlequin Presents® novels and my free surprise gift. Then send me 6 brand-new novels every month, which I will receive months before they're available in stores. In the U.S.A., bill me at the bargain price of $3.12 plus 25¢ delivery per book and applicable sales tax, if any*. In Canada, bill me at the bargain price of $3.49 plus 25¢ delivery per book and applicable taxes**. That's the complete price and a savings of over 10% off the cover prices—what a great deal! I understand that accepting the 2 free books and gift places me under no obligation ever to buy any books. I can always return a shipment and cancel at any time. Even if I never buy another book from Harlequin, the 2 free books and gift are mine to keep forever. So why not take us up on our invitation. You'll be glad you did!

106 HEN CNER
306 HEN CNES

Name	(PLEASE PRINT)	
Address	Apt.#	
City	State/Prov.	Zip/Postal Code

* Terms and prices subject to change without notice. Sales tax applicable in N.Y.
** Canadian residents will be charged applicable provincial taxes and GST.
  All orders subject to approval. Offer limited to one per household.
  ® are registered trademarks of Harlequin Enterprises Limited.

PRES99   ©1998 Harlequin Enterprises Limited

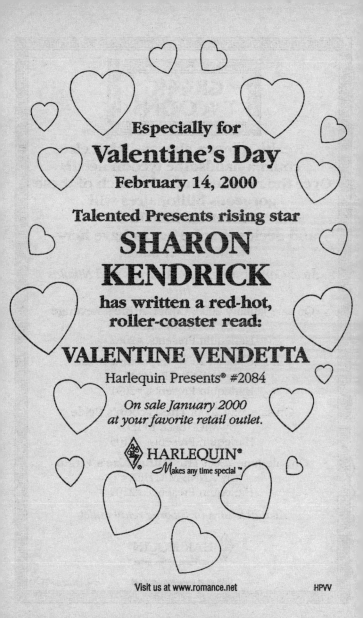

London's streets aren't just paved with gold—they're home to three of the world's most eligible bachelors!

You can meet these gorgeous men, and the women who steal their hearts, in:

NOTTING HILL GROOMS

Look out for these tantalizing romances set in London's exclusive Notting Hill, written by highly acclaimed authors who, between them, have sold more than 35 million books worldwide!

Irresistible Temptation by Sara Craven
Harlequin Presents® #2077
On sale December 1999

Reform of the Playboy by Mary Lyons
Harlequin Presents® #2083
On sale January 2000

The Millionaire Affair by Sophie Weston
Harlequin Presents® #2089
On sale February 2000

Available wherever Harlequin books are sold.

HARLEQUIN®
Makes any time special ™

Visit us at www.romance.net

HPNHG

HARLEQUIN PRESENTS®

SWEET REVENGE *Seduction*

They wanted to get even.
Instead they got...married!

by bestselling author

Penny Jordan

Don't miss Penny Jordan's latest enthralling miniseries
about four special women. Kelly, Anna, Beth and Dee
share a bond of friendship and a burning desire to
avenge a wrong. But in their quest for revenge, they
each discover an even stronger emotion.
Love.

Look out for all four books in Harlequin Presents®:

November 1999
THE MISTRESS ASSIGNMENT

December 1999
LOVER BY DECEPTION

January 2000
A TREACHEROUS SEDUCTION

February 2000
THE MARRIAGE RESOLUTION

Available at your favorite retail outlet.

HARLEQUIN®
Makes any time special ™